NETFLIX

STRANGER THINGS

LUCAS ON THE LINE

OTHER TITLES IN THE STRANGER THINGS UNIVERSE

Runaway Max

Rebel Robin

NETFLIX

STRANGER THINGS

LUCAS ON THE LINE

SUYI DAVIES

Random House 🏠 New York

Jacket art by Ian Keltie
Jacket art and interior illustrations copyright © 2022 by Netflix, Inc.

Text copyright © 2022 by Netflix, Inc. All rights reserved. Published in the United States by Random House Children's Books, a division of Penguin Random House LLC, New York.

Random House and the colophon are registered trademarks of Penguin Random House LLC.

Stranger Things and all related titles, characters, and logos are trademarks of Netflix, Inc.

Visit us on the Web! GetUnderlined.com
ReadStrangerThings.com

Educators and librarians, for a variety of teaching tools,
visit us at RHTeachersLibrarians.com

Library of Congress Cataloging-in-Publication Data
Names: Davies, Suyi, author.
Title: Lucas on the line / Suyi Davies.
Other titles: At head of title: Stranger things | Stranger things (Television program)
Description: First edition. | New York: Random House, 2022. | Series: Stranger things
Summary: "A stand-alone novel about *Stranger Things*' Lucas and his journey of coming into his own personality, interests, and identity".—Provided by publisher.
Identifiers: LCCN 2021060844 (print) | LCCN 2021060845 (ebook) |
ISBN 978-0-593-56787-6 (trade) | ISBN 978-0-593-56788-3 (lib. bdg.) |
ISBN 978-0-593-56789-0 (ebook)
Subjects: LCGFT: Novels.
Classification: LCC PZ7.1.D346 Lu 2022 (print) | LCC PZ7.1.D346 (ebook) |
DDC [Fic]—dc23

Printed in the United States of America
10 9 8 7 6 5 4 3 2 1
First Edition

For Black nerds who contain multitudes

Lucas's guide to surviving freshman year:

☐ *Make new friends*

☐ *Get out of comfort zone and try new things*

☐ *Be yourself*

PART ONE

CHAPTER ONE

I stand in front of my bedroom mirror and hold up two bandanas. One, the usual military camouflage; the other, a polka-dot red-and-white. Both go well with my favorite *Karate Kid* shirt. All I need to do is make a choice.

But this isn't just a choice between two bandanas.

There are only two days of school that matter to me: the first day and every other day. But this is not just any first day. It's the first day *of high school*. First day to make new friends, go out there and try new things. First day as a man. First day of the rest of my life. And I get to kick it all off at Hawkins High.

Which is why I've been stuck here for the last twenty

minutes, thinking in front of the mirror. Do I really want to show up looking the same as I have every day since middle school? If I go to my first day of high school dressed like my old self, I'll just be reminding everyone that I'm still that nerdy kid from AV Club.

And more importantly, every old shirt transports me to some time or place in the last two years when I was scared. Every pair of jeans is a time capsule of the way my friends and I struggled to survive, every pair of shoes a reminder of our summer of fighting to save our families, our teachers, our town.

Today is my first shot at a normal life in Hawkins. No monsters, no missing kids, no Russian spies. The last thing I want is to begin this phase of my life by wearing memories I'd rather forget.

I toss both bandanas in the laundry basket. I take off my *Karate Kid* shirt and throw it on top of my bandanas.

"Breakfast, Lucas!" calls Mom from downstairs.

"Coming!" I scream back.

After rummaging through my closet, I decide on a safer choice: a plain T-shirt devoid of characters, which is just perfect because it says absolutely nothing about me. Plain pants, too. Fresh start, fresh Lucas.

For a moment, I wonder if I should do anything about my hair. But it's too late to start anything now. I did want to do something before, but everything I found in the magazines was all about curls, curls, curls. Even when they mention hair that looks like mine, it's all about Jheri curls.

And I know Dad will go absolutely bonkers if I turn up at the house wearing an eight-dollar Jheri curl treatment. I'll have to be cool some other way. Maybe I'll grab me some of those acid-wash jeans or Jams shorts everyone seems to be wearing these days. After all, one of my rules for surviving this year is to get out of my comfort zone.

I keep my corduroy jacket on, though, because the weather's starting to get fall cool. My choice of shoes is the one stylish decision I make: the Vans Old Skools Max got me for my birthday. Never worn them before. Too Jeff Spicoli. Maybe today's a good day to be more Jeff Spicoli.

On my way out the door, I stuff everything else I need in my bag, making sure not to forget my trusty pocket-size notebook. My hand reaches reflexively for my Wrist-Rocket before I realize what I'm doing. My arm hangs in the air, conflicted. Fourteen whole years, and I've never gone out without my Wrist-Rocket, ever. But today is different. Today is the day I put everything from last summer and beyond behind me. Today is the day I start living in the real world.

The Wrist-Rocket joins the bandanas and shirt in the basket.

■ ■ ■

Downstairs, breakfast is as usual. Dad's behind the paper, Erica's pouring too much syrup, and Mom's teasing her for it. Eggs, bacon, and coffee are the prevalent smells. They occupy much of the table. There's ham, yogurt, and some Toaster Strudels to go with them.

One thing is different, though. Uncle Jack, Dad's brother from Philly, has started his Labor Day visit earlier this year. He sits at the table this morning. Uncle Jack rarely makes breakfast, often preferring to sleep in, but the few times he does, his presence always makes the table seem off balance. Not just because he's the tallest person there—taller than Dad, even—but because it's a four-person table, and we've only ever had four chairs. His presence means more plates, cutlery, and food than usual. It also means Erica's shunted aside, and Uncle Jack's rogue armchair now occupies a good chunk of that side of the table.

The nature of the table changes when Uncle Jack's here, too. On a regular day, it's mostly Mom asking us about any plans with our friends, with Dad looking up from his paper to chime in when he needs to. Sometimes Erica gets on one, and when I have time for her, I respond. But otherwise, the table is mostly a comfortable kind of quiet.

Except when Uncle Jack comes around, he *always* has something to say.

"Ooh, first-day outfit!" Mom says, the first to see me come down the stairs. She claps her hands. "Let me go get my camera."

"Mom, really?!" I sling my bag over the chair, pluck a piece of bacon, and slip it in my mouth. I don't hate it when Mom takes photos. I love it, in fact. But I can't tell her that because then she'll never stop.

"Looking good, son," says Uncle Jack. Dad lowers the paper, peers over it, and harrumphs. He doesn't like it when Uncle Jack calls me son. He says nothing about my clothes, either, which usually means he approves.

"Looking *good*?" says Erica. "Seems to me like someone's overcompensating on their first day." She leans over. "Where's your bandana? Or your Wrist-Rocket?"

"Don't be an—" I look at Dad to see if his view is obstructed by the paper before I mouth the word: *Asshole.*

"Language, son," Dad says from behind the paper.

I make a face at Erica. She makes one back.

"Maybe you think you're like Clark Kent with his glasses," she says. "But even without that bandana, everyone will still know you're a loser."

"Oh, shut up. What do you know about Clark Kent?" I pack some eggs, ham, and Strudels onto my plate, then pour some orange juice into a glass.

"Oh, what, you think I have to be like your nerdy ass to know about superheroes?"

"Language, Erica," says Dad.

Uncle Jack chuckles. "Look at your filthy mouths. You two spend too much time watching movies."

Mom returns with the camera, but puts it aside while we dig into breakfast. I wolf down as much as my mixed feelings about first day will allow. Uncle Jack has come down with his portable transistor radio, which is playing softly in the background. It's tuned to Hawkins FM. Sometimes we get stations from Philly, especially if we go outside, sit on the deck, and plug in to the long-range aerial antenna outside.

"I've been thinking, Uncle Jack," I say. "What happened to the people who didn't die in that bombing you were telling me about?"

"Hmm?" Uncle Jack swallows his coffee.

"Those broadcasts we heard when we managed to get the Philly station a few weeks ago? About some people at Osage Avenue who called themselves MOVE? They were bombed by the Philadelphia Police Department for being too loud or something."

At the head of the table, Dad lowers his paper. Not quickly, like when he wants to say something, but slowly, like when he wants to listen.

"Ah, that," says Uncle Jack. "Government still denies it, you know? Sixty-one row houses, right in the middle of the city. *Sixty-one!* And just like that—*poof!* All for what? Because Black folks loving ourselves is *too loud* for them." He shakes his head pitifully. "Half those MOVE kids are now out on the streets, homeless. Imagine if it was some white folks. First, it'd never have happened; second, if it did, we'd be in a war right now. And I'm sure they'd never leave their own stranded in the streets."

"That's enough, Jack," says Dad in his commanding voice, the one Mom says he learned in Vietnam.

Dad does not pretend to like Uncle Jack. They're brothers, but they didn't grow up together and only rediscovered each other later in life. Dad calls him a rabble-rouser, and puts on his fake Hoosier accent when he says it, so you know he's serious even when he says it jokingly. Whenever Uncle Jack visits, Dad makes sure to complain to Mom whenever he can ("How do I get this man to take that damn tobacco stink and those damn sunflower seeds out of my house?"). He thinks Uncle Jack eats too much for an unemployed person and tries to shuffle him away as soon as he can. Granted, Uncle Jack doesn't have a *job* job—he's some sort of unofficial community leader in Philadelphia—but still. Dad's a bit much when it comes to Uncle Jack.

"Kids need to know these things, Charlie," says Uncle Jack. "Besides, Lucas 'bout to be a man now. You really want him going into the world not knowing his history?"

"*My* kids," says Dad, "will know what I want them to know, when I want them to. And again—I've told you, my name is Charles, not *Charlie.*"

Uncle Jack holds up his hands. "My bad, *Charles.*"

"But, Dad," I interject. "I *do* want to know stuff. What if we leave Hawkins someday? We'll need to be able to fit into the world out there, right?"

"We're never leaving Hawkins," says Erica.

"Uh, speak for yourself."

"I *am* speaking for myself," she says. "Why would I want to leave when I can have everything I want right here?" She shakes her head. "Out there is just competition. I'm not built for that. Nope."

"Nobody's going anywhere," Dad says, then flicks the paper and resumes reading.

It's days like this I remember Dad doesn't love change. Which is why he hates it when Uncle Jack punctures the Hawkins bubble for me and Erica. Dad's completely at peace with me spending a lifetime in Mike's basement playing D&D or video games or watching movies all day, and with Erica chilling in her room with He-Man figures and Barbie dolls. God forbid we even consider life beyond Hawkins. Or worse, talk about it at breakfast.

If only he knew about all the monsters we've hunted or how many times we've been shot at by government agents—Uncle Jack's stories would be the least of his worries. Uncle Jack only tells us the *real* stuff about the world out there, the stuff we'd never come in contact with if all we did was cocoon in this bizarro town. Like these MOVE folks, for instance. I learned a few things in middle school history about slave revolts and all the Martin Luther King stuff, but I've never heard about anything like this. Not in 1985 and so close to home, in the same city where my uncle lives.

It hit me different.

I've been thinking about these MOVE people ever since, thinking about myself . . . how it could've been us. Sixty-one houses just for the color of someone's skin? *Insane.* For all the media reports that have been branding this town *cursed* all summer—and for all the truth in that—no such thing could happen in Hawkins. Or so I think.

"Jack," says Mom, patting his hand across the table. "Let it go."

Uncle Jack shrugs. "Your loss." To me, he says: "Sorry, kid. Maybe you can get that info somewhere else."

After breakfast, Mom takes a few photos of me in the yard, right in the same spot we took my Snow Ball photos last year. I'm still excited for first day of high school, but not as pumped as back then, and Erica doesn't help by snickering the whole time. Afterward, we wait for Mom to pull the car out and drop us off. Uncle Jack comes by while we wait, draping an arm over my shoulder.

"Got any plans for today?"

I shrug. "Make new friends? Survive the first day? Have fun?"

"Good choices," says Uncle Jack, then leans in and whispers, "Best think 'bout hanging out with kids like yourself, though. Make up for what you missing at home."

CHAPTER TWO

MONDAY, AUGUST 26, 1985

Mom drops Erica off at the middle school first, then me next. The ride feels like it takes forever, but soon, the familiar parking lot of Hawkins High School comes into view. I've never really thought about how flat it looks, compared with the middle school, which is shaped like a massive barn. This also means everyone can see everything, including freshmen getting dropped off by their parents on the first day.

I slouch in my seat and hang my head, trying to get below the window level. Mom shoots me a look and I sit back up straight.

"There's nothing to be ashamed of, Lucas," she says.

"Plenty of high schoolers get dropped off by their moms. Mrs. Miller from two streets down drops off her daughter. Also, Mrs. Harris down the same corner. Drops off her son and two of his friends. They seem fine with it."

"I'm sure they'd rather take the bus." I look out the window. "At least pull over here, lemme meet up with Dustin and Mike before I walk in. You want me to go in alone on my first day of high school?"

Mom shakes her head but agrees and pulls over. She tries to kiss me on the forehead before I leave. Nope.

The parking lot teems with people, drowns me in sounds. Unlike middle school, where it was either bus or bike if you weren't dropped off, now there's students arriving in their own cars—loud, abrupt, some almost doing wheelies as they park. It's the most people I've seen in one place since that ill-fated Fourth of July carnival. A flashback to that day hits me: the screaming, the sound of shaking trees, the pound of the Spider Monster's feet, blood—so much *blood*. So many people gone, so easily.

I stop in my tracks and shake it off, bring myself back to the present. But even in the present, I'm lost at sea, unsure of where I'm supposed to go next. Then I realize there's only one set of front doors anyway, and just follow the mill of students heading that way.

I find Dustin just where I'd predicted—at the bike rack on the veranda. It takes a while for me to recognize him at first, because, while I thought I'd had a whole makeover,

Dustin had a *whole* makeover. Now he's peering into the mirror of his bike and adjusting his hair.

"What the hell is *that*?"

Dustin's hair, which was already big, is now even bigger. Maybe because he isn't wearing a hat to cover his curls this time. Without it, what he's done to his hair is very clear. He's blown up everything, trying to go for a mullet. It looks like a bad perm.

"Good hair," Dustin says. "The kind that gets you noticed for all the right reasons."

"Lemme guess. You're taking advice from Steve Harrington again."

"Who says it's Steve?" Dustin pats at the hair, as if that'll make it shorter or less curly. "And so what if it's him?"

"That'll explain why you look like a discount Jennifer Beals."

"Hey! I did everything like before. Wash and condition with Fabergé Organics and—"

"Four puffs of Farrah Fawcett hair spray, yes, you have explained this *multiple* times. It didn't work out for you at the Snow Ball, and ten bucks says it's not going to work out for you now." I shake my head. "Man, you're seriously tripping. How can you not see that you're missing the most vital ingredient?"

"Which is?"

"You have to be born with the right hair in the first place, Dustin!"

Dustin scoffs. "Bullshit. Anyone can get good hair, born with it or not. I just need more time."

"Yeah, maybe your definition of good hair is the problem, man."

"What's that supposed to mean?"

"Never mind," I say.

"Well, *you've* made some changes too," he says, pointing to my bandana-less head. "Face it. We both know high school is brutal, and we're both trying to make sure we start on the right foot."

"Fair," I say. "I'm just trying out a few changes, though, not a whole makeover."

"A *few* indeed," says Dustin. "This is as close to a makeover as you get, Lucas." He leans forward and pats at his hair again. "Maybe it'll work out this time and girls won't sneer at us." He stops. "Not like we're looking for girlfriends, of course. I've got Suzie, Mike's got El, you've got Max."

As soon as Dustin says her name, I realize I never spoke to Max about hanging out on the first day. It's been a while since we talked, anyway. *One* more part of my life that needs fixing.

"Yeah, right, that," I say. "Not sure Max and I are in the same lovey-dovey place you guys are, though. It's been weird with us since Starcourt. *She's* been weird."

Weird is an understatement, really. The summer of the Flayed did a number on the whole party, even on the whole town. We're all still crawling our way back to normal. Not Max.

"Well, that sucks," says Dustin. "I wish I could say I can relate, but I can't." He pauses for dramatic effect. "Because, you know, I've got—"

"A genius girlfriend, yes, Dustin, we know."

Nancy drops Mike off. She waves to us from afar before shuffling off to rendezvous with her partner at the school paper, some guy named Fred Benson. Dustin and I wave back. Like most of us, Nancy's been MIA since Starcourt, everyone dealing with the tragedy in their own way. Mike says she's buried herself in college applications and is making plans for her impending long-distance relationship with Jonathan. Mike also says she's been irritable, but none of us wants to tell him that *he's* the irritable one.

Mike already wears his ready-made scowl as he comes toward us. Unlike us, and expectedly, he has made no changes to his appearance. Not even to his general moping, which began from the second we learned that Will and El will not be joining us for the school year because the Byerses are moving permanently to California. El's going with them. Right after the Starcourt debacle, they left with Dr. Owens to go make arrangements for their new living situation. We haven't seen or heard anything about them for a while—for safety reasons or whatever. That and the general gloom of the mall disaster has turned Mike into the worst person to be around.

"Hey," Mike says.

"Really?" says Dustin. "*Hey?* On today of all days?"

"Not in the mood, Dustin."

"You know they're still going to return and pack up the house, right?" says Dustin. "You're still going to see her. At least try to exist as a human being before then?"

"Yeah, whatever." Mike turns to me. "Want to go to school or what?"

I shrug.

"Cool," says Mike. "See you at homeroom or something." He goes through the doors.

"Happy first day of high school to you, too, Mike," Dustin calls after him. "What an asshole." He leans forward, taps some more at his hair, then gives up. "Fine, *fine.* I guess this will have to do."

CHAPTER THREE

MONDAY, AUGUST 26, 1985

High school is off to a rocky start.

I assumed that I'd be in the same homeroom with Dustin and Mike, and probably Max. And since we have pretty much the same interests, we could all select the same classes and end up spending all our school days together.

Wrong.

Every face looks new to me, even though I know a bunch of these kids from middle school. But in here, they don't look the same. They are dressed different, act different, speak different. Studded jackets, hoop earrings, screaming makeup, Argyle sweaters, Gap hoodies, Guess jeans. There's even one guy in a Champion turtleneck.

Worse, they all pretend like we're complete strangers. I don't go up to anyone just yet, but their body language says it all. Those who're dressed alike quickly find themselves in groups, a binding energy wrapped around them. Their glances scream to everyone outside of that group to stay away at all costs. It's like they have all been infected by some kind of parasite that makes them assholes. I can't help but remember the Mind Flayer, and for a moment, think of high school like it's some kind of mind flayer itself. How it's making everyone suddenly become something they aren't.

I sit at the back of homeroom with my thoughts, close to the door so I can leave quickly. Our homeroom teacher, a tall man with a mustache who introduces himself as Mr. Lansdale, talks on and on about the day's agenda and some spiel about how to take notes in orientation and classes. Little of this is new to us former Hawkins middle schoolers with older siblings (or friends with older siblings), so only a few people seem to be paying attention—I figure these are the new students. My gaze goes around the class, trying to determine who is who. But I note how not a single one of these fellow former Hawkins middle schoolers will even look me in the eye, or acknowledge that we once shared space in the same building. It's like I don't exist, like I'm in some kind of upside-down version of life before high school.

It takes me a while to notice I'm the only Black person in the room.

I can't remember the exact moment I started unconsciously counting how many Black people were in a place when I went out. Sure, places like Uncle Jack's Phila-delphia or New York or Mom's hometown in Virginia have tons of Black people in one place at a time. Not Hawkins, though I didn't really notice that until after the MOVE thing. I even began to wonder how many places with many Black people have been bombed before—I know Uncle Jack said that was why their headquarters were targeted. Thankfully, there's never more than four Black people in a room at the same time in Hawkins (and four only happens when it's all the same family). Chances of being bombed—slim to none.

Afterward, Mr. Lansdale takes us into the hallway to show us our lockers and how to use them. As I fumble with my locker, I spot Max in a group with another homeroom teacher who's showing them how to set up their combina-tions. I wave at her. She meets my eye, lifts the corner of her lip in a half smile, but doesn't wave back.

Okay, I was not completely honest with Dustin. Max and I are in a very not-great place, and it seems like it may be getting worse. She's been spending a bunch of time alone since El left, which I understand. But she's also been canceling on me a lot lately. Even the few times we've hung out, it always felt like she was physically there but mentally elsewhere. And the challenge is that I can't tell if this is about Billy's death or about her mom or her stepdad (or her mom *and* stepdad). She doesn't talk about any of that much, and changes the subject when I ask.

I wonder if maybe she's tired of having me around.

Maybe I'm not cool enough for her or something. Maybe she's trying to change in high school too. Whatever is going on with her, I at least have a right to know.

I store her locker number in my memory and plan to leave a note for her later.

Next, Mr. Lansdale shepherds us to the orientation assembly. This one is in the massive auditorium, and I'm happy that I finally get to sit with Mike and Dustin. But, nope. We are required to sit with our class groups. I spot Dustin in his Weird Al shirt all the way up in the front. He's getting harangued by students from his group for his over-the-top hair. Some boys are reaching over to pull at it, while the girls giggle. Mike hangs his head next to Dustin, helpless, while their homeroom teacher tries to regain order. The sight makes my heart beat faster, and I clench my wrists. I feel guilty that a part of me, somewhere inside, is glad I didn't end up in their homeroom after all.

I settle in with the kids from my class, trying for an end-row seat so I can leave early and catch up with the boys after. But of course, the end-row seats are occupied. Seems I'm not the only one trying to run out of here as soon as I can. I'm sandwiched between a bunch of kids I don't know.

Might as well make new friends. That's part of my plan anyway, isn't it? Especially since the next two hours seem like they will be super boring anyway. I can already tell because the vice principal is flipping through a thick binder and calling us to attention at the podium.

"Hi," I say to the boy seated next to me, extending my hand. "I'm Lucas."

The boy, dressed in a Lacoste knit sweater I could've sworn was handmade, looks me up and down. *Actually looks me up and down!* Then he shakes his head. *No thanks.* Without another word, he turns back to face the podium.

I clench my fists harder to prevent my hands from shaking.

I've never been the shy type. Not in the usual way, at least. And maybe I'm not good at talking to girls or being the coolest guy, but I've always found that when it comes down to it, I can hold my own. But so much has changed over this past summer and early fall. Between all those people dying, our party abruptly breaking up, feeling Max start to slip away—I've not been feeling as confident in myself as I used to. I was hoping that high school would help change that. Apparently not.

I spend the next double period preventing my neck from turning my head in the boy's direction again. Principal Higgins starts out with some forgettable spiel that I vaguely remember contains staff introductions (I don't remember a single teacher's name), attendance rules, dress codes, all that stuff. When he gives the speech on anti-bullying, there's a funny moment when another teacher mimes what we shouldn't do by shouting mean jokes at an empty chair and grabbing it like it's a person. That's hilarious. Everything else—pretty drab.

Afterward, we each get a folder containing our schedules,

student IDs, and the cafeteria menus. We're also made to wear little name tags.

"For the next period, you'll be meeting your one-to-one peer mentors," Mr. Lansdale says as we disperse after. "Make sure you're at the designated location on your timetable in the next few minutes."

I finally reconvene with Mike and Dustin, who are poring over their own timetables.

"Well, about time," says Dustin. "What the hell is all this about having us in separate homerooms?"

"Can we talk to someone about it?" I ask. "Should be easy to fix, right?"

"Does it matter?" asks Mike, though he sounds less mopey now. High school's already working its magic on him. "We'll just sign up for the same stuff anyway and spend the rest of the day together."

I tilt my head. *Fair point.*

"Who'd you get for peer mentor?" asks Dustin. "I got someone named Cason Walker. God, I hope he's not a loser."

"Gunner Lane," says Mike, reading his schedule. "Sounds cool. Maybe he even rides a Harley."

"Pfft," says Dustin. "As if anyone in this town could be *that* cool."

I look at mine and find a surprising name: *Jermaine Demario.*

"Interesting," I say aloud. The warning bell for next period rings.

"We better get to it," says Dustin. "Meet up in the cafeteria to pick classes and extracurriculars together?"

"Yup," I say, but my mind is elsewhere, steps ahead of me and already at the English room where I'll be meeting my peer mentor.

CHAPTER FOUR

MONDAY, AUGUST 26, 1985

Jermaine Demario is the first Black boy I've *seen* at Hawkins High.

He's a good-looking one too. I'm not sure where that thought comes from, but it just pops out at me. Maybe it's because I've always had a different idea of what *good-looking* means compared with my friends—especially for someone who looks like me. Jay's the right kind of tall, probably up in the sixes. He has long legs, struggling to fit underneath the table between us now, so that he has to lean, one arm over the back of the chair, giving him a cool edgy look.

And there's his hair.

I'd never really understood what all the fuss was about Steve Harrington's hair. I mean, sure, it's great and all. It has to be, since even buried under that goofy hat, it was still the reason more girls trooped into Scoops Ahoy than was normal. It's all Dustin croaks on about, what he considers the definition of cool. But I guess I had to see Jermaine's hair to understand why Steve's never quite did it for me in the same way.

Jermaine's hair is an Afro curl that goes over the front of his head and down the back, but not in a Lionel Richie type of way. More natural curls, less product. He's shaved the sides down so that it looks like a mohawk, but instead of bald sides like the punks who hang out at the skatepark have, his is just a buzz undercut that's overflowed by his curls. It's the coolest thing I've ever seen, and a few of the girls in the room agree. Freshmen and upperclassmen alike, they all cast side glances at him.

And something even better: he wears a basketball jersey over a T-shirt. *NBA All-Star,* it says.

"You play basketball?" is the first question I ask when I sit down in front of him. He laughs at how forward it is.

"Lucas Sinclair, is it?" he says, then extends a hand. "Jermaine, but you can call me Jay." We shake hands, and his eyes twinkle. "Straight shooter with the questions, I see."

"Sorry, sorry," I say, embarrassed. "It's just . . ." I pause. "I haven't really seen—"

"Black guys at Hawkins High?" He smiles out of the corner of his mouth. "Ten bucks says they paired us for that very reason."

We laugh.

There's an easiness to the way he speaks. His coolness has the opposite effect on me than the more popular kids' usually does. Instead of pushing me away, it opens up the room, asks me to be free with him, to be myself.

It strikes me now: *This* is who I want to be. This is *how* I want to be cool—like Jay. I wonder what it takes and if I have it.

"I thought the same thing on my first day too," he's saying. "Came in as a transfer student halfway through freshman year, so it's a bit different from your experience right now. Didn't get no orientation, no peer mentor, nothing. So all I wanted was to know—where did all the Black boys hang out?" He smiles. "But you'll find out, like I did, that just because we aren't all gathered in one place doesn't mean we don't exist."

"I guess," I say. "Crazy, though."

"What is?"

"That you're a jock." I've only ever seen Black players in the NBA on TV, but never as *jocks*. The idea is surreal to me because I've simply never seen a jock who looked *exactly like me* before.

"You *are* on the basketball team, right?" I ask him.

"I am," he says, amused. "Dunno if that makes me a

jock, though? At least, not in the way you mean it. Jason and the others, maybe, but not me."

"To me, if you're on the team, then you're a jock and a popular kid. It's how high school works."

He laughs. "If you say so. I guess you could technically say I'm on the team. Now, if only I could get off the bench and break into the starting lineup."

"Oh." I'm taken aback. "That's surprising. You look like you could be a good player."

"What—cos I'm Black?"

His directness jars me. "No—no, I mean." I point to his jersey. "I'm guessing not-great players don't just wear All-Star jerseys?"

"Ha." He chuckles. "Don't sweat it, I was just messing with you. But you'd be surprised to know that back in Cleveland where I'm from, people just wear these for fashion." He pinches his jersey.

"For real?"

"Yes. And to your question—I'm a decent player, if I do say so myself. Was in the JV front lines at my last school. But all the starting guard positions here at Hawkins High are locked in for the season, and Coach's not going make some rando sophomore a starter." He shrugs. "No biggie, though. I'm patient. I'll get my time." He leans forward. "But enough about me. If we don't talk about you, I don't get the extra credit for this session."

We start where the orientation package suggests: tips for navigating high school, favorite subjects, plans for the rest of the semester. I tell him about my guide to surviving freshman year.

"Ah, I like that," he says. "Here's three you should add." He motions for me to take them down. "One: avoid relationship drama." He pauses. "Got a girlfriend?"

"Yeah? Kinda?"

"Whatchu mean *kinda*?"

"Like, yes, we're dating, but it's kinda weird right now. Some stuff happened over the summer."

"Well, that stuff better be unhappened real quick, cos it'll consume your life if you let it. Same thing with any friendships you let run rogue. If you want to survive—really survive—you balance your classes and extracurriculars with any other part of your life, else one monster swallows the other, you know what I mean?"

"Yeah." More than he knows. I scribble.

We talk a bit about science stuff, and I tell him of my time with AV Club and the science fair. He nods along and doesn't mention *nerd* or *freak* once. Not even when I tell him about D&D, which he knows a bit about, though he's never played.

"What about you?" I ask. "What do you like?"

"Just about anything that interests me?" he says. "Basketball, music, reading—I like to go wherever my heart goes."

"Except maybe Cleveland, Ohio," I say jokingly. "Must have not been great if you left it to come to this cursed nowhere place."

A small cloud comes over him then, a slight shift in

his temperament for the first time. Kind of similar to how Max's mood shifts when anyone so much as mentions Billy's name.

"I'm sorry, that was a dumb thing to say."

"No, no, that's okay." He smiles a wan smile. "Tell me about this cursed-town reputation. What's all this in the news about chemical spills?"

After registering how swiftly he's changed the subject, I tell him the media-sanitized version of how the Hawkins Lab event and the tunnels led to our cursed Independence Day and the Starcourt fire. Nothing about the truly cursed things that happened and how the media's not too far off in their speculation. As I speak, he leans back and listens intently, a frown on his brow. I hope I'm not scaring him. If, despite everything that's happened, people like Jay and his family are still attracted to Hawkins, then maybe it's not as bad as it seems after all.

"This town, man," Jay says after. "I knew this place was crazy when that fire happened, but, whew, looks like that was just the tip of the iceberg."

We return to the orientation package's prompts and talk about extracurriculars. I explain my plans to join the resident D&D club, which my friends and I have heard is called Hellfire.

"Oh," he says. "I thought you were interested in basketball. The way you talked about my jersey and everything."

"Oh, no, I'm no good at sports," I say. "I don't even,

like, know the rules of basketball. I just thought it was cool to, like, you know, be talking to a jock and whatnot."

He snickers. "Again, I don't consider myself a jock in the traditional sense of the word."

"Well, you're cool like the rest of the team. You're on a first-name basis with them, right? I'm sure if you hit that starting place you mentioned, you'll be just as popular, if not more."

He shrugs. "Well, that's what hanging around the popular kids will get you, I guess." He tilts his head. "If you ever end up thinking basketball is cool, though, maybe you should try out for the team. We'll have a table over in the gym with the other clubs when extracurricular sign-ups begin. Come by then?"

I'm too shocked by the invitation to respond. *Me? On the basketball team? Doing what exactly?*

"No thanks," I say. "It's Hellfire Club for me."

He shrugs again. "Whatever you say, man. But if you're going by your own survival guide—*get out of your comfort zone, try new things, make new friends*—then nothing says you can't be both Hellfire guy and basketball guy."

"That's *impossible*, Jay. No one can be a nerd *and* a jock."

"Says who?"

"Says . . . everyone?"

He snorts, rising just as the bell for next period goes off.

"Well, there you are, Lucas. Pro tip for high school: all the rules are made-up, and the only rules that matter are the ones you make for yourself. Just . . . try not to get in your own way?"

He leaves me with directions to the next room on my schedule, but I barely register them. *Try not to get in your own way* has burned a mark into my mind, and for a long moment after he leaves, I hear it loop in my brain, over and over until it becomes a wordless mush, like a tape caught in the stereo.

CHAPTER FIVE

MONDAY, AUGUST 26, 1985

Lunch period is rowdy. There is a long line of freshmen spilling out of the cafeteria and into the hallway. Apparently, we all spent too long with our peer mentors. Were we all fascinated by them, or was that just me?

I join the line of bustling students, craning my neck over multiple heads to see if I can spot Mike, Dustin, or Max. I see Dustin's hair and T-shirt before registering that he and Mike are already in the cafeteria. They're seated at a table, alone. They're looking around—likely for me, maybe also for Max. I wave, stretching so they can see me, but they don't. Dustin's too busy writing something in his folder, and Mike is spinning a faded dodecahedron die from an old D&D set. I step out of the line and head for them. Maybe I can leave my stuff at the table and get back in line for my food.

As I approach, a group of boys—upperclassmen, from the look of them—saunter past their table. They look like trouble. One of them whispers something to another, watching Dustin. The receiving dude passes on the message to another, and soon, all of them begin to snicker. Then one leans in close to Dustin, who is too busy writing to notice, and Mike's too focused on spinning his die to see what's happening.

"Nice perm," the boy says into Dustin's ear, then pulls at his hair.

Dustin jumps, startled. The boy begins to ruffle his hair, and Dustin swipes, trying to get his hands away. Mike gets involved, and his die spins, skittering off the table and onto the floor. One of the boys kicks it into the opposite corner of the room. Everyone at the adjacent tables laughs.

I slow down, clenching my fists for the third time today. Memories from middle school bubble up, interplaying with the scene before me: getting beat up for winning the science fair, for being in AV Club, for being a *freak*. It's almost like we never left, like we're trapped in a world with no escape. It hurts even more because no one tells the boys off. The laughter just increases now that others are looking up and taking notice. Maybe they think we deserve it. We're only a bunch of nerds, after all.

Eventually, the boy lets go of Dustin's hair, laughing as he leaves with his squad. Mike stares daggers at them but stays put because they're real big, real tall. Even Dustin, often the first to open his big mouth, gives the boys a long look and decides against speaking. I bet it's running through both their minds now—El's not here to save them this time. I bet it'll hit Mike harder, knowing she might be gone for good.

It makes me feel even more guilty for waiting until the upperclassmen leave to approach the table. Dustin has patted his hair back into place, and their long faces have settled.

"Hey," I say, trying to be cheerful. They don't need to know that I saw what just happened, and I don't need to make them feel embarrassed that I did. "What's with the long lines? How did you guys get food?"

"Showed up early," says Dustin, back to his nonplussed self. "I hear that's the only way to not spend all of lunch period in line. Didn't your peer mentor tell you that? Mine did."

Before I can respond, Dustin's moved on. "Anyway, I was just telling Mike that I hear the head of Hellfire's this stoner named Eddie Munson. I hear he's . . . intense."

"Your peer mentor tell you this, too?"

"Of course," says Dustin. "I asked all the proper questions. Anyway, listen, with this Eddie guy, I'm thinking we have to, like, declare our intentions early. He doesn't sound like someone with a lot of patience. We might not have the luxury of waiting until next week to sign up at the extracurricular showcase." He leans forward. "I'm thinking: What if we get our names in early? Like, today?"

"Don't be silly, Dustin," I say. "Hellfire's not going to get full anytime soon. Tell him, Mike."

Mike just shrugs. There's a part of me that's happy for this brooding Mike, a shadow of the scrappy, in-your-face Mike I've known all my life. Mopey Mike is like an upside-down version of him, complete with the negative vibes even when he's just sitting there, doing nothing. But a part of me remembers my friend's still in there somewhere. He might be too stubborn to admit it, but he needs our help dealing with this El and Will moving situation.

I put a hand over Dustin's scribbling to stop him. I love Dustin, but gosh, he can be so aloof sometimes.

"Why don't we just—breathe, for a moment?" I pantomime breathing in and out. Both of them look at me quizzically.

"Listen, how about a big movie night this weekend? Your dad finally put the TV and VHS player in your basement, right, Mike? Dustin, you could go to Family Video and rent something good—two movies, maybe. Max and I can pick up some pop, and, Mike, you can get popcorn. Just us and movies, all night." I clap my hands. "What you say?"

"Yeah, my dad's not gonna like that," says Mike.

"Your dad doesn't like anything," I say.

"True," Mike agrees. "But I'm not sure my mom's

gonna be happy either. She's not going to let Max stay over. Says girls are not allowed."

"Well, I think we can argue that there's four of us, so if they're worried about making out and stuff, that's not going to happen, right?"

Instead they stare at me.

"That's going to be *your* call, chief," says Dustin.

"Wow, Dustin, ew, disgusting," I say. "I would never just make out in the middle of movie night. That'd be gross." I turn to Mike. "But does that mean we're on?"

"Maybe," he says finally. "I'll ask Nancy, see if she can help soften my parents up. We'll have to bribe her, though."

"Fine, I'll pay," I say. "If that's what it takes to have *one* fun night."

"Guys," says Dustin. "Not to rain on the movie night parade, but I think we should be taking this Hellfire sign-up seriously—"

"Hellfire can *wait*, Dustin," I cut in. "Besides, it's not the worst thing in the world if we don't get in. We'll simply find something else."

Mike and Dustin look at one another, then burst out laughing.

"You're kidding," says Dustin. "You've got to be kidding."

"What do you mean?" I say, Jay's words coming back to me now. "We can try new things. Isn't that what we agreed high school's all about? Like, what if I wanted to try out for the basketball team?"

Now they laugh even harder. Dustin's folder falls over to the ground, and Mike wipes his eyes. Their laughter's directed *at* me, but it's the first I've heard them laugh like this in a long time. Especially after what just happened five minutes ago, it feels like they deserve it, so I let them make me the butt of the joke.

CHAPTER SIX

THURSDAY, AUGUST 29, 1985

I don't catch up with Max until the middle of the week. I left a note in her locker yesterday, inviting her to movie night. I asked her to respond by slipping a note in mine, but there was nothing in my locker when I checked this morning.

After school, I take my bike ("No more drop-offs for me, Mom—I'll manage, thanks!") and search for her in the three places I know she's bound to be if she isn't at home. I don't find her at the arcade, which is both surprising and not. Everyone's thinking about change, and Max is no different. Maybe there's a part of her that realizes, just like the boys and I have, that the kids in the arcade are getting younger and younger, and we're looking older and older standing next to them.

Next spot is Benny's Burgers, which hasn't been open since El first showed up in Hawkins and Benny died. Max goes there whenever she wants to be alone and if she doesn't want anyone to find her. It's a long ride, and when I arrive, the place is shut tight, empty. Peeling boards, shattered glass, and dust cover the floors, over which I can see multiple footprints crisscrossing each other. A favorite spot for the kids from Hawkins High, judging by the cigarette butts, beer cans, and joints smoked down to as far as little fingers can hold them. Everything I expect is here but Max.

So I try Max's third spot—Elmore skatepark.

It's not technically a skatepark. At least not like the cool kind Max describes from California, the ones from movies that look like a meteor dropped and left a concrete crater. Elmore looks more like someone started digging a canal and changed their mind halfway through. It's just a large ditch surrounded by a wire fence, with random graffiti painted in it, many of them referencing someones or somethings named *Cab* and *Hawk* along with a lot of crudely drawn boobs and penises.

And then there's the skaters themselves, always dressed in jeans or leather jackets, wearing weird hats and berets, earrings on one ear, always a boom box nearby, blaring metal or garage bands. Skating isn't really a thing in Hawkins, but even though summer is technically over, the skatepark is full of punks. They pretend to be tough, but I don't think they scare anyone. I'm pretty sure if I paid attention, I'd realize it's all the same eight or ten kids from down the road who laze around, trying to be different. This is the closest thing to West Coast vibes we get down here in Hawkins. Max escaping here makes sense.

When I find her, she's not skating. Just sitting on the edge of the concrete barrier, watching. She seems to do a lot of watching these days. I drop my bike in the grass and shuffle up to her.

"Hey," I say, waving. "Get my note?"

She looks up. "Yeah."

"Oh, okay," I say. "I wanted to check."

"Okay," she says.

"So you'll make it? To movie night?"

"I'll think about it, Lucas."

I take a deep breath and settle in beside her. She seems surprised by the action, which surprises me.

"Come on, Max," I say. "I know you miss El and maybe you're waiting for her to come back before you start to hang out again. But we all have to find ways to live without those who are gone, you know? Besides, the Byerses are only coming back for a day, and we'll probably only spend it packing."

I say *those who are gone* because I know what mentioning Billy does to her. I hope she gets the message, regardless.

Max frowns. "What does this have to do with any-thing?"

"I'm just saying. Movie night might be good for you."

"And I said I'll think about it."

"Okay, okay." I sigh. "I want you to know . . . you can talk to me."

She looks at me directly. Something inside me warms up, and for the first time in a long time, I'm reminded of her small blue eyes, sharp but sensitive. I'm reminded of that mix of intensity and tenderness. Her sincerity—toward herself and others—was always the reason I was drawn to her in the first place. These days, I feel like that's what's slipping away the most. Those bright eyes look dim and tired now.

"Yeah, I know," she says.

She doesn't follow that up with anything, so I let the sounds of the skatepark settle between us. Boards lifting and dropping, plastic and rubber wheels slapping concrete, shoes scuffing and squeaking. Some thrash metal song blaring from the lone boom box. The swoosh of a skater sailing by. The occasional grunt of someone falling.

"I'll try and make it" is all she says after.

■ ■ ■

On my ride back home, I finally come to terms with the feeling I've had all summer: that a part of Max died on the Fourth of July.

I mean, people *died* died. Hopper, for one. The Holloways, Mrs. Driscoll, along with a bunch of other Flayed people. Across town, there's not a single person who doesn't know someone who knows someone who lost someone to the summer. And though the news reports softened everything up by saying that what happened was a chemical spill, it still didn't stop the deaths from hitting us hard.

Max is the only one among us, the inner circle, to have witnessed the death of the person she lost. She always said she didn't consider Billy family, but there's something about seeing a person die before your eyes. I will admit I absolutely hated Billy for how he treated her, how he treated me. But standing right there, watching the Spider Monster dig into his chest like he was a throwaway mannequin—it still gives me nightmares.

She cried a lot that night—and many days after—and there was nothing I could do but try to be there for her. A part of me wanted to be upset, to say, *Billy made your life a living hell.* When she later told me something he once said about me being bad news for her, it made me even angrier. He didn't know me, but thought I was a problem? And what did he base that on? A part of me thought maybe he deserved what happened to him, that maybe the Mind Flayer chose him as a vessel for destruction because he already had so much darkness in his heart. Because Billy was a destroyer himself.

But no one deserves to die like that. And no one deserves to watch that happen to family.

I've tried everything I could to get Max to come out of the black hole she fell into that day. Hangouts. Movie theater dates. I even volunteered to go over to her house, since she won't come to mine. But she still hasn't let me visit her at home. Even now that Billy, the main reason for her keeping me away from her home, is gone, she still won't let me come by.

I could be wrong, and she may just be as mopey as Mike is over El leaving. I get it. They've been real close since the summer—closer, even, now that they've both lost someone. Between Max's parents' divorce, her move away from California, and Billy's death, El leaving is yet another new space opening up in Max's life. I understand it can't be easy.

But I'm her boyfriend, so it's my job to show her I can help make that space not feel so empty. All she has to do is let me in. And all I have to do is try harder to open that door.

CHAPTER SEVEN

FRIDAY, AUGUST 30, 1985

Somewhere between my movie night idea and Nancy's failed attempt to get the Wheelers to agree to Max joining us, the event has been recast as a slumber party of sorts. Apparently, the only way to get Mrs. Wheeler's mind out of the gutter about what might happen with a teenage girl sleeping in her basement was for Nancy to paint some picture of us reenacting the pillow fight from *Annie*. Imagine all of us singing "It's the Hard-Knock Life." That did the trick, but also completely changed the course of our night.

Mrs. Wheeler agreed for Max to stay for the movie, but not the slumber part. However, she was so excited by the idea of a fun sleepover that she designed a whole new program. Now, in addition to seeing the two movies Dustin got—*Planet of the Apes* for us and *The Karate Kid* as my surprise for Max—we're set up for an indoor camping party, complete with glow-in-the-dark bubbles, cupcakes (which Mrs. Wheeler is baking herself), and a "not too loud, boys" pillow fight. *Maybe it'll help him stop being so foul,* she'd said, gesturing toward Mike.

I'm not mad, actually. Pretty sure we may not get another weekend like this for a while. From what I hear, the first week of high school is the only free time you get to screw around. After that, it's pedal-to-the-metal hard work. Unless, of course, you don't care about grades, which I don't have the luxury of doing while I live in my parents' house.

So I take my job, getting the soda, seriously. During lunch period, I leave a note for Max to meet me at Bradley's Big Buy after school. There's no note confirmation in my locker by the day's end, but I don't give up. After school, I rush home, grab a quick snack, then call her house number, hoping maybe someone—anyone—will pick up. As usual, no one does.

I bike over to Bradley's on my own, crossing my fingers that I'll see her there. But that doesn't happen either. I decide to do the shopping myself.

First order of business is the caffeine that'll help us stay up. For myself—and myself alone—I get New Coke. And since everyone else thinks I'm somehow crazy for liking it, I get them all Jolt Cola instead. To mix it up, I get a couple of Slices and Squeezits in different flavors, and throw in some Fruit Roll-Ups. Luckily, it doesn't go over budget.

Back home, I call Max's house again. Nothing. I call Mike's house, and over clanking dishes and what sounds like a kitchen riot, Nancy picks up and informs me that Mrs. Wheeler has corralled Mike and Holly into helping her bake. Holly has decided to make herself useful, hence the clanking. Seems like everything is going okay with everyone except Max.

I call Max's house a third time. Someone picks up and growls an unfriendly hello. I can almost smell the alcohol in his drawl.

"Hello, Mr. Hargrove," I say. "I'm Lucas Sinclair, Max's friend. Is she there?"

"Maxine does not live here," he says, "and she wants nothing to do with you." Then he hangs up.

■ ■ ■

Movie night is meant to be fun. We set up four tents in Mike's basement, one for each of us—Mrs. Wheeler insisted on separate tents. But the fourth remains empty all night because Max never shows up.

I don't call her house again, but I ask Nancy if there's a chance she or Mr. and Mrs. Wheeler know anything about the Hargroves. No dice. During the movie, I tell the boys what Max's stepdad said about her not living there anymore.

"Shh," says Dustin, chomping on popcorn. "Here comes a good part."

"You think they moved or something?" I ignore him.

"Without telling us?" asks Mike.

"And without Neil? And without telling her boyfriend?" Dustin glances at me, incredulous. "Dude, seriously."

So I lie in the tent for the rest of the night, eating popcorn and cupcakes and trying to enjoy *Planet of the Apes.* And I do enjoy most of the party, even the cupcakes and the pillow fight. But I still worry about Max the whole time. I know Mr. Hargrove—*Neil*—is not exactly the most trustworthy person. Max has been keeping me out of her house for a reason, and I feel like he's the number one reason why.

Tuesday's the only opportunity for me to see her—the first school day after Labor Day. So when the long weekend crawls to a close, I bike to school with vigor. Before homeroom, I hang back in the hallway for as long as I can, hoping to catch Max before going in. No luck. I leave yet another note in her locker.

At lunch period, I'm stuck in line—*again*—while Mike and Dustin have found both seats and food. But that's the least of my worries. All I'm doing is stretching my neck, trying to see if I'll somehow find Max here, probably having lunch on her own.

I'm still looking around when a hand falls on my shoulder. I look up at Jermaine's face.

"Hey, man." He fist-bumps me on the shoulder. "Having trouble getting food?" He clicks his tongue. "Don't worry, I gatchu."

Before I can respond, he glides over to the lunch lady and has a few nice words with her. She laughs, then places food into two trays for him. He offers her a mock bow, then balances one tray on each hand, tiptoeing his way back to me. Both our lunches have a cheeseburger in them, but for sides, his has chicken nuggets and mine is a pizza. Lunch hasn't changed much since middle school. The only new thing is the fruit-in-syrup cup we both get.

"Yo, wanna sit at our table?"

I follow the direction his finger is pointing in, and stop still.

Sitting at the table are the upperclassmen jocks from the first day, the same ones who messed with Dustin and Max. I didn't think of it then, but now I look at them close, realizing they're just the right kind of big to be shoo-ins for the basketball team. Probably fellow subs with Jay, since I didn't immediately recognize them as players.

"Uhhh . . ." I wonder how someone like Jermaine can sit at the same table as these bullies. I bet he would tell them off if he knew what they did.

At this point, Mike and Dustin have spotted me standing with him and are staring straight at us.

"Those your friends?" asks Jay.

"Yeaaah, kinda."

"Oh, I get it. It's okay if you want to sit with them."

I scratch my head.

"Or, you know, whatever you decide," says Jay. "I'll be over there." He walks over to join the table with the upperclassmen.

I stand there, a deer in headlights. The choice before me momentarily wipes all thoughts of Max from my brain. Before me sit Mike and Dustin, watching, maybe even wondering what decision I'll make. Behind them, at the end of the aisle, the chance of a lifetime: a cool table, with basketball players. But more importantly, a table with the coolest Black boy I've ever met, and the only one I know in Hawkins High.

Best think 'bout hanging out with kids like yourself, Uncle Jack had said. *Like yourself.*

I remember being upset when Uncle Jack said this, because I knew he was talking about the Party—he'd spotted Will, Mike, Dustin, and me together a couple of times. I'd always thought of us four as *exactly* alike—and in many ways, we are. But standing here, in this moment, those two words—*like yourself*—replaying over and over in my brain, it *clicks.*

Now it's even clearer how different my friends' lives are from mine. How I once would have *died* to be teased for long, curly hair like Dustin's, but can't even if I wanted to. How *cool* means something different for me than it does for them—whether they're talking *nerd cool* or *popular cool.* How, no matter where we go or who I am or who I choose to be, I'll always be *the Black one* standing next to them.

Not that it's their fault or anything. But that one hour I sat with Jay was the first time I didn't feel defined like that. Instead, I felt a certain kind of freedom—that I could be anyone, anything. I haven't felt that way in a long time, and it was exhilarating. I want to feel like that again, now and always.

So, standing in the middle of the cafeteria, tray in hand, I see myself having a seat at both tables. Jay's table is not just any table—it's *also* a popular one, which means I get to sit next to jocks—one of them *just like me!* A golden opportunity, falling into my lap, right at the beginning of high school. The odds of this opportunity knocking again soon are really, really low.

But my friends and I have been through the toughest things. Attacked by monsters, shot at, underground, aboveground—we have always stuck together, and this is how we've survived. Maybe survival in high school will be the same.

I force my legs to move, the decision playing in my head.

"So, after lunch period, we're heading to the Hellfire table . . ." Dustin is saying to me as I approach, then trails off. "Lucas . . . ?"

"Sorry," I whisper over my shoulder as I breeze past them, my expression as apologetic as I can make it. "I'll explain later."

I don't look back. I know exactly what their own expressions will be.

At the jock table, the upperclassmen are laughing at something Jay said. They stop short when they see me standing there. Jay, whose back is to me, turns around, spots me, then scoots over.

"Right, here you go," he says, patting the seat. As I sit, he says to the others: "Boys, this here is Lucas, my peer mentee. He's gonna try out for the team."

"Bitchin'," says one of the boys, Mark, I learn—the one who kicked Mike's die. He lifts a hand and daps me up. The others follow suit, each high-fiving me in return. One of them asks if I'm anywhere as good as the NBA Rookie of the Year, but Jay silences him with a cutting look, which is great because I have no idea who that guy (someone named Michael Jordan?) is.

I look back at Mike and Dustin's table. Their backs are already to me. Some guy with long hair, dressed in distressed jeans and a heavy metal band T-shirt, stands at their table, speaking to them. He looks scary, in a weirdo way.

I keep looking in their direction, hoping they'll turn around and I can apologize with my eyes. *This is explainable. I can explain.*

But they don't look.

CHAPTER EIGHT

TUESDAY, SEPTEMBER 3, 1985

I'm not sure how many minutes are left before the bell rings for the end of lunch period. I pick at my food and plan to slip away from Jay's table so I can catch up with Mike and Dustin and explain everything. Before I can extricate myself from arguments about who can stuff the most Skittles in their mouth (answer: Mark, 104 Skittles), they've gone off with the long-haired heavy metal dude.

I mumble something to Jay about needing the bathroom and make my escape, barely noticed by anyone else at the table. As I roam the hallway in search of my friends, wondering if I've made the right decision, I notice some new arrows have been planted on the floor and walls. They all point toward the gym.

Extracurricular sign-ups, they read.

Right. Completely forgot about that.

The gym is full of freshmen when I arrive, scattered around the floor and bleachers, but mostly congregated around various tables with club banners over them. Each club has gone wild trying to attract and recruit new blood. Drama Club has a huge photo of some archaic guy that could be anyone from Dickens to Shakespeare. Marching Band has hung instruments from the ceiling and has one of their uniforms on a mannequin so that students can get a photo standing next to it. The wrestling team has done a similar thing with their singlets. Science Club's table has a cool mini-lab setup with beakers and pipettes and whatnot, Chess Club has a chess set on theirs, and the school newspaper has, well, newspapers.

There are two kinds of tables that get no lines. The basketball team's the first. I'm guessing because no one is stupid enough to risk ridicule and attempt to sign up for tryouts if they've not already been invited. Unless they're really good, in which case they'd already be in cahoots with the team anyway, like the two freshmen I spot approaching the table.

I'm not sure if I could call what they've set up a *table* in the traditional sense, since no one is sitting there. It's just a sign-up sheet and a pen. Not even a banner or sign. But everyone recognizes it by looking at the seniors standing around in their letterman jackets. And, of course, the basketball they're tossing among themselves. I count about nine boys in jackets, three of them Black. Plus Jay, who's four. Plus me, who makes five. It's the most Black people I've ever seen together in one place here. Maybe even in town. It's a bit jarring to witness.

"Hellfire Club," a freshman walking past me says, reading a banner to another freshman. "More like freak association." They giggle.

I turn to the direction they're focused on.

The Hellfire Club is the other kind of table that gets no lines. It has a banner that's hard to miss. Unlike the other banners, it's handmade instead of printed. But it's especially notable because it looks like a death metal album cover: aggressively edgy and emblazoned with fire and devil horns, with the club name scrawled across it.

Mike and Dustin are the only two people standing there. The long-haired dude from earlier is seated behind the table, chatting with them. This must be Eddie Munson, the stoner Dustin spoke about the other day, leader of the official Hawkins High D&D club. Or, as it's clearly going to be known by everyone else soon: the Freak Association.

"Lucas," says Dustin, who has spotted me, and whose abnormally loud voice always carries no matter where he is. "Sonofabitch—"

He and Mike scurry over to me. Somehow we end up meeting halfway, right in the middle of the court. Out of the corner of my eye, I spot Jay and the other jocks arriving at the basketball table and shaking hands. Jay speaks to one of the jacketed boys, a preppie-looking Hollywood-type dude—team captain, is my guess. Then Jay looks up, points in my direction.

Oh boy. This will *not* be good.

"What the hell is wrong with you?" Mike has suddenly regained his appetite for anger. "You left us at lunch to go sit with . . . *those guys?*"

"They're assholes, Lucas!" echoes Dustin.

"I know, I know. I said I was sorry."

"*Sorry?* For blowing us off and camping with the enemy, you think *sorry* is gonna cut it?"

"Well, technically, not all of them are our *enemies*—"

"Did you see them being jerks to us?" Mike asks.

I don't want to lie, but telling the truth will make my decision seem worse than it is. I opt for the middle.

"They were?"

"Super jerks," Dustin chimes in. "One yanked at my hair. God, high school is just middle school raised to the power of ten, isn't it?"

"So—what, you're like—friends with them now or something?" asks Mike.

"No, not *friends,* no. It's . . . complicated."

"Uncomplicate it," says Dustin.

"Jay's my peer mentor, and he wanted me to sit with him at lunch." It's not really a lie, but it stretches the truth just far enough.

"*Jay?*" Dustin scrunches up his nose. "What the hell's a Jay?"

"It's short for Jermaine. Listen, I said it's complicated, and I've apologized."

"Whatever." Mike shakes his head. "Look, we're signing up now, and we've been talking to Eddie about our past campaigns. Come. You need to meet this guy. He's got to meet everyone before they can sign up."

Mike grabs my arm and wants to pull me along, but something else happens then.

"Lucas!"

It's Jay. Hand raised, he's calling me from the opposite end of the court. The jacketed boys around him, captain included, follow his gaze . . . to *me*.

Oh no. I freeze. *It's happening.*

Mike and Dustin have noticed. And they're not pleased.

"Is that this Jay person?" asks Dustin. "Tell me he's not a jock too."

"And why's he calling you over . . . ?" adds Mike.

I open my mouth but struggle for the words to say, *Sorry, guys, I'm trying out for basketball.* But I don't need to. The way their faces change tells me they've put it all together.

"Oh my God, Lucas," says Mike. "You've got to be kidding me."

"Listen, I didn't really plan to try out for the team or anything. He just asked me, and I thought, *Why not?*"

"*Basketball*, Lucas?" says Dustin. "Really?"

"It's just a tryout. And it's not like it's going to take the place of Hellfire or anything—I'm still joining, aren't I?"

"Can you even throw a ball?" Dustin looks me over, as if seeing me anew. "You? Hoops and nets and whatever?" He shakes his head. "I don't see it."

Maybe it's the tension of the moment, or the anxiety of my dilemma. Maybe it's Uncle Jack's words replaying in my head. Maybe it's just the way Dustin says it, shaking his head with disgust.

"What is that supposed to mean?" I counter, suddenly miffed.

"Lucas, we've been friends since forever," says Mike. "I've never seen you go near a ball, not once. And now you want to try out for *basketball*? Sounds more to me like you want to try out for *jock*."

"So what? How d'you know I don't have other interests?"

"Do you?" asks Dustin. "That'll be *news* to me."

"There are a lot of things about me that'll be news to you, Dustin," I say. "To both of you."

"Now, what's *that* supposed to mean?" asks Mike.

I shake my head. "Forget it." Something stubborn stiffens in me. "But this is happening. Last I checked, I don't need your permission to do anything or be anyone."

I turn away before they can fashion a response. Long-haired Eddie Munson, who's kept his eye on us the whole time, leaves the table and comes up to them.

"That the Sinclair dude you spoke about?" I hear him say as I leave. "Let him go, let him go. Better to have no one than someone who doesn't want to be here, right?"

Jay's talking to the captain when I approach. He's a blondish boy with a perpetually amused expression, as if there's always a sly game he's playing.

"Jason, this is my peer mentee, the one I was telling you about, Lucas Sinclair," Jay's saying to him. "Wants to sign up for the team."

"That so?" says Jason, angling his head and looking me over. "Not very tall, though, are you?" He leans forward and pokes at my biceps. "Skinny, too."

"Yeah, yeah, which freshman isn't?" says Jay.

"Fair," says Jason, then to me: "What position you play, Sinclair?"

My heart stops. My heart rate quickens.

"Uhhh . . ."

"Guard, right?" says Jay, then angles his head just slightly, as if to say, *go on.*

"Yes," I say. "I believe so."

"One or two?" Jason presses. Before I can look lost again, he answers the question himself. "Probably a one. You're too short to be a two, and you don't look like you can shoot."

He whistles sharply at the other boys passing the ball between themselves. Then he points to me. Without warning, the jock with the ball turns and pulls the ball close to his chest in his two palms.

"Think fast!" he says, firing the ball at me.

Of course I don't think fast. My body takes control, a combination of me flailing to protect myself, while also trying to catch the ball. It slams into my hands, large and heavy, and almost ends up in my face, mere inches from my nose. By some strange stroke of luck, it doesn't fall.

"Nice catch!" says Jay, almost as if trying to mask the truth that I am absolute shit at this. *Why is he helping me?*

"Okay, okay," Jason is saying. "Not good, but not terrible, either. Here's another one: Can you pick the ball up with one hand?"

I frown. "That's . . . impossible?"

Jason laughs. The other jocks laugh with him, including the subs from the cafeteria table earlier. The only person who doesn't laugh is Jay. He's giving me a measured gaze, as if to say, *Go on, Lucas, you can do this. Show them.*

I place the ball on the ground, instantly anxious. And when I get anxious, my arms start to shake, which isn't great for what they're asking me to do. But I try to focus, flattening my palm against the ball, gripping it as much as its roundness will allow. No luck. The ball is *humongous.* My fingers scrape across its surface. The boys snicker even more.

Come on, Lucas, I think. *This is your one chance to change your fortune in high school. Don't waste it.* I lean closer to the ball, spread my palm over it. *You fought and defeated the Spider Monster. Don't let a little round ball defeat you.*

I grip the ball as hard as I can and pull up.

My eyes bulge as the ball leaves the ground and follows my hand up. Even the jocks are surprised—their laughter dies down slowly.

This moment of triumph doesn't last long, though. The ball slips from my hand just as quickly as it stuck to it. My fingers snap together as the ball leaves, bouncing toward Jason, who catches it, then nods.

"That's a five out of ten," he says. "Not my cup of tea, but Mr. Theo will freak if he hears I turned an underclassman who isn't absolute garbage away from tryouts. Especially a freshman like . . . *you.*"

It takes me a moment to clock that his *like you* is exactly the same as Uncle Jack's *like yourself.* I look to Jay to confirm if I understand what's just been said. Do they think I'm a shoo-in for tryouts just because I'm . . . Black?

But Jay wasn't listening. He stands off to the side, engrossed in conversation with one of the jacketed boys.

"Anyway, good luck with it," says Jason, before signaling to the boy Jay is talking to. "Patrick? Let the skinny kid sign up."

Patrick, who's one of the few Black seniors and the only one in a jacket, hands me the sign-up sheet. Only two names on the sheet so far—probably the freshmen I noticed earlier. Nobody else in my grade is near the table. From the look of things, it doesn't seem like there'll be more sign-ups for tryouts. If *elite club* had a description, this would be it. And somehow, I've crawled my way in.

When I thought *change,* this isn't really what I had in

mind. But I'm also unable to contain my excitement for all the possibilities this future holds. *Lucas Sinclair on the basketball team! A high school jock! A popular kid!* My hands are shaking from the thought. So much so that when Jay hands me a pen, I'm unable to write my name, so he does it for me, gently inquiring if *Lucas* is spelled with a *c* or with a *k*.

"Welcome to the club, homie," Jay says once he's done, passing the clipboard back to Patrick and slinging an arm around my shoulder.

The bell goes off to end lunch period. The gym starts to clear out.

Over at the Hellfire table, I can see Mike and Dustin watching me. I stare back at them, a blender of emotions roiling within me. I'm irritated that they thought I couldn't be anything more than the Lucas Sinclair they know—that just like Dad and everyone in high school and Hawkins, they'd prefer if I remained the same kid they've always known. I feel triumphant for proving them wrong. And though I have absolutely no idea how I'm going to impress at tryouts without any skills, this is not really about basketball.

This is about finding someone who can relate to my exact experience as Lucas Sinclair in this high school, in this town. It has taken me *years* to find *one* such person— Jay—and it'd be foolish to let our friendship evaporate before it even begins. That's something my old friends will never truly understand.

As we stand there, Jay's arm still on my shoulder, my

eyes track over to the Video Game Club's table. Standing there is Max. But she's not looking at the sign-up sheet in front of her. She's looking right at me.

Relief washes over me. *Okay, so Neil was just lying and being an ass.* But my unease creeps back up as Max's gaze continues to linger. She squints, searching my face, as if she's trying to recognize me but for some reason cannot.

That's when it clicks: I must've changed too much.

Something in my chest caves, because she's right. I've always known it wasn't just a part of Max that died on the Fourth of July. All of us, in our small ways, lost parts of ourselves that summer. I wish I could go back to being that innocent boy in middle school who didn't care about girl-friends or basketball or saving Hawkins from monsters and Russian infiltrators. But that boy died that day too. And I don't know who this new person is. None of us do.

The only thing we know is that everything's changing, and nothing will ever be the same between us all.

Lucas's guide to surviving freshman year:

- ☑ *Make new friends*
- ☑ *Get out of comfort zone and try new things*
- ☐ *Be yourself*
- ☐ *Avoid relationship and friendship drama*

PART TWO

CHAPTER NINE

WEDNESDAY, NOVEMBER 27, 1985

Thanksgiving break of '85 makes a strong case for being the shittiest one ever. The weather's not great, and Mom won't let Erica and me go outdoors alone. She's been listening to all those conspiracy theories about satanic cults invading Hawkins. Apparently, somebody decided that devil-worshippers must have had something to do with the Starcourt fire and Hopper's death. Mom's become so paranoid about letting us go anywhere alone that sometimes, I just feel like breaking protocol and telling her the truth: the only Satan she needs to worry about is governments— ours included—infiltrating Hawkins, opening gates into dimensions filled with monsters. Either way, she insists on resuming dropping us off at school, among other places. I can go out only if I'm meeting with friends, which, for a while, I didn't even have.

I didn't speak to Mike and Dustin for weeks after I signed up for basketball trials. Nine weeks and three days— I counted. We avoided each other at school, and they went to D&D and made new friends with upperclassmen. I got stuck with nothing, since JV trials don't start until basketball season in December. Luckily, I've had Jay, who decided to take his peer mentoring a step further, coaching me on the basics of playing basketball. We've been spending more time hanging out both in school and out, and it's helped cushion the blow of losing my friends.

But then Jay noticed how distressed I became whenever we spotted them at school, and after asking me about it, said: *Keeping grievances too long hurts you more than it hurts them.* By some stroke of luck, Nancy was saying the same to Mike at home, poking at his hard shell. But Mike and I are stubborn, so we did nothing.

Luckily for us, Dustin is the opposite and quickly became bored with the whole situation. He asked Steve Harrington for advice, and Robin Buckley, Steve's coworker, overheard and volunteered to play independent mediator for the three of us.

Two and a half weeks ago, we sat together for the first time at a table in Family Video and hashed out our differences for hours, Robin acting as referee whenever things got too heated. Since then, we've returned to being cautious friends, not quite back to where we were before high school began, but on our way there. To get things *there* faster, we've decided to do something fun, and settled on our first movie night in forever.

But we know the fun will be a bit sour because Will, El, and the Byerses have finally moved out of Hawkins.

It's been about a month now, but I still remember the day they returned to pack up the Byerses' house. We cried, all of us—even Mike, who likes to act tough. And when the U-Haul pulled Joyce's lemon-green Pinto into the dust, we stood there and watched. I knew *everything* would change for good.

And change it has.

Mike went straight back to moping, but it's even worse than before. He won't come out of the house; he won't go anywhere. He's in his basement all day, playing *Super Mario Bros.* on his new Nintendo Entertainment System. When he's not there, he's writing letters to El, now that he has her California address. Mrs. Wheeler can't even get him to leave his room these days. That means that the Party—if we can still be called that—has not spent any time together since.

Dustin isn't helping either; he'd rather spend his free time radioing all day with Suzie. Especially now that he's retrieved Cerebro from Mount Weathertop and refitted it to the roof of his house. Cerebro 2.0, he calls it. I have no idea what they talk about all day long, but I'm sure that's not how having a girlfriend should work.

Speaking about spending time with girlfriends, I could kill for some of that right now. But Max, like Mike, has retreated further into herself since El left for good. And even though Mike and Dustin are slowly coming around to the idea of me joining the basketball team, Max surprisingly hasn't. She thinks it's stupid that I wear sweatbands and carry a ball everywhere. I tell her it's not intentional—*I'm just always practicing,* I say whenever she takes a second to listen to me. I hear that Mr. Theo, the JV assistant coach who makes the final picks for the feeder squad, does not play favorites.

I think that Max uses basketball as an excuse to be angry at me. Something is definitely up at home with her. She still won't let me come over for anything, not even studying. She won't talk to me about her parents, or explain why her stepdad said she doesn't live at her house anymore. There's always some new excuse for her to disappear on her skateboard, and the few times we talk, it always ends in some shitty argument. I hate that more than anything.

So it feels like a coup when she agrees to join us for movie night *and* come with us to select the movies at Family Video. We decide to meet on the Wednesday before the long Thanksgiving weekend.

Nancy drops Mike, Dustin, and me off in the parking lot—another one of Mom's conditions of the outing. It's humid for November, and though the sun is not scorching, it feels damp, as if the weather is offended. We're all offended right back. Not a great way to start the day. Mike is lethargic, Dustin is high-strung and restless, and Max isn't even here. If this is a warning sign that something is going to go wrong, it sure is making itself known.

"Did you have to bring *that* with you?" asks Dustin, pointing at my basketball.

My friends might have come around to accepting that I may join the team, but that hasn't stopped them from showing their disapproval whenever they can. Especially because Eddie Munson, supreme leader of Hellfire Club, recently declared that there was no longer room for new sign-ups in Hellfire until the spring semester. Which means Dustin and Mike are stuck in Hellfire without me for a while, and they have not been taking it well.

"Jay says I need to get familiar with the ball," I say. "And I can't get familiar if I don't hold it often, can I?"

"This is *us* time," says Dustin. "Not basketball practice."

"Just say you're jealous I'm spending time with Jay."

"Jealous?" He snorts. "Have you *seen* my girlfriend?"

Mike and I roll our eyes.

"I'm just saying," Dustin continues, ignoring us, "you called this together, right? In my head, *we* are going to Family Video to hang out, and then have movie night later. If there's one day to leave your ball at home, it's today. But oh, what a disaster it will be if Mr. I'm-going-to-be-popular is seen without his ball."

I shake my head. "You know if I fail at tryouts on Monday, all my plans to be a part of the team are gone, right? Like, for good. And then I'll be clubless. Imagine that—

first semester of high school with no extracurriculars and no new friends. What worse way to start?"

"Uh, *we're* your friends," Mike chips in.

"Yes, but remember we agreed to make *new* friends and try *new* things? I seem to be the only one keeping to that promise."

"I dunno," says Mike. "Maybe I'm fine with how much *new* is in my life right now."

We fall into silence. I get it. Change is like a coin with one really great side and another really terrible side. Toss it, and you never know which way it's going to land.

Perhaps my coin is lucky; I've fallen more on the good side of change than, say, Mike or Max. Hanging out with Jay has had good effects. Like, *really good.* The kids who didn't want to speak to me on the first day? They say hi in the hallway now. Even girls! I know I have a girlfriend and all, but we haven't really felt like girlfriend and boyfriend for a long time. I won't lie: I love the attention hanging with Jay has brought to my life.

The biggest win of them all has been the complete disappearance of bullying. It makes sense that since jocks do most of the bullying at our school, they understand that I'm now off-limits. No more randomly screaming *Freak!* at me. No more tripping me down the hallways. No more cornering me in the corridors outside the gym.

I know that it must be hard for Mike and Dustin to watch me get special treatment while they're still getting bullied, so I let them jab at me for it. But that's what I've been trying to explain to them all along! If I get on the team proper, it's good news for all of us. They will become untouchable just for being my friends. But they somehow fail to see my perspective. First, because they're convinced that I have no shot of making the team (they may not be wrong) and second, because they say they're never going to stop being nerds, and the jocks will always remember that (also true).

But what kind of friend am I if I don't try?

"What movies are we getting?" Mike asks.

"Toss up between *Conan the Destroyer* and *The Empire Strikes Back*," says Dustin. "We still need to vote on it, though."

"Not a chance," I say. "I told you—Max has been very clear that she will absolutely refuse to see any horror flicks until further notice. I still say we check if *The Last Dragon* is out on VHS."

"Yeah, listening to Max is how we didn't get to see *Fright Night* in the theater, or *Re-Animator*," says Dustin.

"And she's not even here," says Mike.

"She'll *be* here, she's just late," I say.

"And stop trying to make *The Last Dragon* happen," says Dustin. "If we must watch a martial arts movie, I say we do *The Seven Samurai*."

"Well, *I* want *The Last Dragon*."

"Why? Did Jermaine Demario put that on your curriculum too?"

I shoot Dustin a side look, in part because it's kinda

true. They've seen me reading the book he lent me—*A History of the Negro in America*—and heard me talk about the new Air Jordans. But *The Last Dragon* is different.

When I told Jay about my love for all things Daniel-san and Mr. Miyagi, he asked if I'd ever seen a Black karate film before. He told me about *The Last Dragon,* and I was wonderstruck by the possibility of both things coexisting. I've wanted to see it ever since, but I don't want to go to the theater alone. The movie feels like the kind of thing you want to enjoy with someone, with *friends.* But Max, Dustin, and Mike don't seem to think so.

"If we can't agree, maybe we should just let Steve pick the movie," says Mike.

"No!" Dustin and I chorus.

"If working in a video store and having absolutely shit taste in movies had a name, it'd be Steve Harrington," Dustin says.

"Robin, then," says Mike. "Because all this arguing is giving me a headache."

"Don't worry, we'll wait for Max, then we'll take a vote," says Dustin.

CHAPTER TEN

SATURDAY, OCTOBER 12, 1985

The first time Max and I met up after Will and El left, it was at Palace Arcade in mid-October. I found her sitting there, not touching any single machine—not *Dig Dug*, not *Donkey Kong*, nothing. She just watched everyone play. And I had no choice but to sit there with her.

I should've known that whatever was going on with her wasn't just a blip, that things were about to turn even more sideways. I know Max's life has always been tough, even before Hawkins. And though Billy was the one who made her life a living hell—and for some time, *my life*—a part of her struggled with losing him, though she tried so hard not to show it.

As we sat there, she began to talk, for the first time.

Not *to* me, more like *at* me. She gazed into space and talked about San Diego and how she once tried to run away to LA to be with her real dad. She talked about Nate Walker, a friend she'd left behind in California. She talked about how her stepdad had become even more of a dipshit since Billy died. She talked and talked and talked.

I didn't listen much. The whole time, I fumed silently. When other high school kids hang out with their girlfriends, I don't think they sit around and listen to them gripe. They make out and mess around and walk hand-in-pocket on the sidewalks and sit at the back of the movie theater, giggling in the darkness as they eat out of the same popcorn bowl.

Instead, Max has only visited my place one time. My parents were nice, but I could tell from the way they cast glances at each other that they had thoughts. Thoughts they would likely discuss in whispers behind their closed bedroom door. I knew it would involve the two words *Black* and *white,* but I never thought about Max and me that way, just like I've never thought about why we don't act like the other kids in relationships. It's what makes us special: we defy tradition. Sure, we kiss, but we're also best friends, and we depend on each other.

Maybe Max hasn't come over because she picked up on my parents' skepticism. Then again, she wouldn't let me come to her house either. Not even after Billy was no longer there to throw a fit about her hanging out with me.

She insisted that her stepdad, Neil, was two times as bad. *I'm not a wuss, I'm not afraid,* I told her, but she said: *You should be.*

So when she was done talking in the arcade, I said nothing but "Uh-huh." Then I asked her if she wanted to see a movie.

She was silent for a long time. Not angry silent. More like *you don't understand what's happening, do you?* silent. And to be honest, no, I did not understand.

In many ways, I still don't.

But she shook her head, and to my request for the movie, said: "Sure."

When we hit downtown, the Hawk was showing three films: two old ones—*Godzilla* and *Fright Night*—and one new one—*Commando.* I'd been *dying* to see *Commando* since forever. It was everything I loved put together. Tiptop military gear and equipment: check. Explosions: check. Arnold Schwarzenegger swinging through a mall, driving a Caterpillar, shooting bazookas: check, check, check. I'd been going wild at every single preview since.

But for some reason, Max simply looked at all three movies and said: "No."

I did a double take. "No?"

"No." She sounded so much like El with her one-liners.

"Why not?"

She shook her head. "I don't want to watch anything with monsters in it."

"*Commando* doesn't have monsters," I said, incredulous.

"There are always monsters, Lucas," she said. "Even when they don't look like it." Then she walked away.

I ended up seeing *Commando* alone, seething through the entire film. Max's statement stuck with me. I remember wanting to stop her and say: *I understand. I have monsters too.* Some monsters we share—the summer of loss, the pain of El and Will moving—some are hers alone to bear. And there are some that belong only to me. But I was too upset to see that most of us had lost only a few things. Max was losing *everything*.

My plan today is to make up for all that when she comes to Family Video. Just like I'm getting Mike and Dustin to come around, I want Max to see that I'm trying. That I want her to be okay, and that everything I'm doing is to show her how much I care.

CHAPTER ELEVEN

WEDNESDAY, NOVEMBER 27, 1985

We push the door to Family Video and go in. It pings, and Robin looks up from behind the counter.

"Henderson!" she announces, lifting her hands in an imitation of Steve's usual greeting to Dustin. Then she angles her head toward the back and calls, "Harrington! Your children—" She stops to eye us. "Your *teenagers* are here!"

Family Video has changed a bit since Starcourt. Looks like it took the mall to remind them that people in Hawkins like cool stuff after all. So they've gone ahead and expanded the main area. It's no longer just rows upon rows of shelves stacked with VHS cassettes. Now there's a spot with seats where folks can order food from the counter and just hang out. Salted popcorn and a Slurpee seems to be the most common combo, judging by the crumbs everywhere. "Summer of '69" filters across the store from a stereo nearby, playing so low that I can barely hear it. A few people sit at the tables and play the free board games scattered around the shelves. There's a movie on too, muted as it plays on all the TVs stacked around. Always an old one we've seen a million times. Today, it's *Footloose*. From the expressions on a few people's faces, they're likely watching it for the first time. Amateurs.

"Hey, it's the Scoops Troop!" Steve Harrington emerges from the back. He and Dustin clap each other's shoulders. He attempts to do the same to Mike, but Mike inches away.

"You know the Scoops Troop was just you guys and my sister, right?" I say. "That's not us."

"Saviors of Starcourt, then? What are you calling yourselves these days?"

"Oh, oh, I know this one," says Robin, jumping over the counter and sitting across it. "The Party, right?" She tilts her head. "Kinda Orwellian, now that I think of it. Dark, even for you nerd types."

"We don't call ourselves anything," Mike says.

"Yeah, we haven't been a party in a long time," says Dustin. "Thanks to *some* people."

"Don't start," I say. "You guys are the ones who never come out."

Mike shakes his head. "I'm gonna go set up a board game while we wait for Max," he says, walking to the shelves.

"What's wrong with him?" asks Steve.

"The usual," says Dustin. "LDL."

"What?"

"Long-Distance Longing," says Dustin. "Not to be mistaken for my LDL, Long-Distance Love, which—"

"Which Suzie and you have," we all chorus.

"Yeah, yeah, whatever." Dustin gets peeved whenever anyone reminds him of how much he brags about Suzie. "I'm going to go find my own movies. You guys have the new *Star Wars*, right? And the new *Conan*?"

"That's a negative on *Star Wars*, Henderson," says Steve. "Keith's order went in late, so we're still waiting on the delivery." He points toward the horror shelves. "You can check for *Conan the Destroyer* over there."

Dustin walks off triumphantly. I'm left alone with Steve and Robin. Steve eyes my basketball, then without warning, slaps it out of my hands. It bounces, and he catches it, feigning a dribble or two.

"Gah, I miss the ol' days," he says, tossing the ball from hand to hand. "Say, Sinclair, wanna hit a one-on-one in the parking lot?"

I look from the ball to Steve Harrington. *Absolutely the hell not.* I may be trying out for the team, but I'm not stupid. He may have graduated, but I remember exactly who Steve was as a varsity player. Asshole to a hundred percent.

"I'm good, thanks," I say.

"Your loss," he says, then dribbles out the door.

"Harrington!" calls Robin. "Your shift isn't over!"

"So cover me!" he calls back, then is out.

Robin shakes her head. "What a dolt." Then she looks to me. "Anything I can help you with, Lucas? Anything *in particular?*"

I shoot a quick glance at my friends. Dustin is still over by the shelves, and Mike is selecting a board game from the racks.

"Not now," I say, giving her a quick pointed stare. "I'll come back. When *they've* gone." I angle my head toward my friends. She chuckles.

"You know you can just tell them, right?" she says.

I look at my friends. *Yes, but . . .*

"They're not ready," I say.

"Or maybe *you* aren't ready," she counters.

The door opens. I look back to see if it's Max, but instead something hits me in the shoulder, drops to the ground, and rolls away. My basketball. The thrower, Steve Harrington, is sweating.

"Look sharp, Sinclair," he says, panting. "You're gonna flunk tryouts with reflexes like that."

I pick up my ball and stuff it into my backpack, then join Mike and Dustin at the table. Mike has dumped one of the new Trivial Pursuit card games and started to lay it out. We've played this game at least once each time we've hit Family Video since the summer. It's the only thing we play together now that we don't do D&D campaigns in Mike's basement anymore.

Dustin arrives, holding two VHS tapes.

"Ooh, you're gonna love this," he says. "*Conan the Destroyer,* but also, guess what I found? *The New Kids!* Ha! Look here—'from the director of *Friday the 13th.'*" He glances at me. "I bet these'll cheer Max right up."

I have my doubts, but I just let them start the game.

We begin playing, and soon we're so engrossed that we've forgotten why we're here. The game takes an hour and thirty minutes, and we completely lose track of time. Only after we hear someone honking furiously in the parking lot—Nancy, back to pick us up—does it dawn on us that Max never showed.

Mike and Dustin leave with the two films Dustin selected, and I let them because I can't argue for Max if she's not here. I promise to see them at movie night. Nancy wants to know if I'm riding back with them, but after a moment's thought, I tell her I'd rather walk to her house. She's not convinced, but I insist, so she leaves me in the parking lot.

I make sure they're gone before I turn around and head back into Family Video.

CHAPTER TWELVE

Back in Family Video, my eyes dart around, checking to make sure no one with a chance of recognizing me and reporting back to my friends is around.

Steve Harrington sits at the front desk. His brow furrows when he clocks me.

"Forget something?"

"Uh, no." I look behind him. "Where's Robin?"

His confused expression turns inquisitive. "What d'you need Robin for?"

I feel the urge to tell him off like Dustin often does, to say *nonya business*. But Steve and I don't have that kind of relationship. Also, I'm not built to be that kind of rude.

Luckily, Robin emerges from the back room and saves me the trouble.

"Out of my way, Harrington," she says. "Let those who know movies talk movies."

Steve rolls his eyes, shakes his head, and walks away. Robin watches him for a while, making sure he's not looking our way or paying attention.

I quickly retrieve the VHS tape I'm here to return—*That Championship Feeling: 1983 NBA Playoffs and Finals*—and slip it across to her. She receives it but doesn't drop it in the box marked *Returns*. Instead, she tucks it into a private bag.

"You know," she says, "if you ever need any help talking this out with your friends . . ."

"No thanks," I say. "I got it."

"Do you, really?" She angles her head. "Doesn't look like it from where I'm standing."

She leans forward. "Listen, Lucas—I know high school's a big change and every little thing can feel like a big deal, like your whole life is always about to fall apart. But believe me—your whole life will be just fine. Even if it doesn't feel like it will."

She's not wrong. Mike and Dustin have been upset with me for so long—and me back at them. Then Will and El returning for *one day* brought us all back together, and suddenly everything was forgiven, like we hadn't spent weeks avoiding each other. Even Max and I, who hadn't spoken in a while, were excited to be hanging out for the first time in forever. But now they're gone, and things have settled back into their old place. Not completely, though. We may be back to being friends, but they still raise eyebrows at me splitting our usual hangout times to practice basketball with Jay.

Some part of me thinks they may be jealous, but I can't really blame them. I'd be jealous if they were jocks. Which is why I'm keeping this from them. I'm not sure they're ready to know just yet that the reason I often have to bail right after school and miss some of their *Super Mario Bros.* sessions is because I'm watching basketball tapes Jay recommended. I'm not ready for them to be upset with me again so soon.

"It's been . . . tough," I say.

"Wanna talk about it?"

I look up at Robin. I haven't spent any significant amount of time with her, but from the little I have, she seems like one of the smartest people I know. Maybe not grades-type smart, but I see her reading all the time, both at school and up here at the counter. If she was a few years younger, she would've fit into our party, easy. I'm not surprised that she sees right through my nonanswers.

In fact, rather than wait for an answer, she motions me over to an empty table. We sit, facing each other. I only just now realize how many freckles she has, which is, like, a bazillion.

I pull out the small notebook where I jot things down. It was a present from Dad one Christmas that had always lain there unused until now. Seemed like a good place to lay out my plans for the year in writing, among other things, like lessons from basketball practice with Jay and notes from the tapes. Also: plans for stuff to do with Max once things get better between us.

"Ooh, a diary," Robin says, motioning to the spiral binding and small pen attached to the flap. "Look at you all fancy."

"What—no, no, it's not a diary. Just some short notes I like to keep. Look." I show her my guide to surviving freshman year. Unsurprisingly, she stops to study my notes with interest.

"Ah," she says. "I see why there's trouble in paradise." I look to see if she's kidding around, but she has her face scrunched up in genuine concern.

"What is it?"

She jabs a finger at the second line I've marked as completed. "See where you say *Get out of comfort zone and try new things*? That's great, on its own. But then, remember *you* are also someone else's comfort zone. So when you start making new friends and trying new things . . ."

It clicks. "They start to feel . . . jealous?"

"Well, I wouldn't say *jealous*. More like their own comfort is threatened, you know? That's an expected side effect of change. Every new thing you try takes the place of one that used to be there before. And when what's replaced is something you share with friends you've known your whole life, it can feel like a betrayal. But the way they're feeling and the way you feel are both completely normal." She clicks her tongue. "You'll all get over it, eventually."

"Like, when?"

She shrugs. "Long as it takes. All change takes some adjusting to."

I consider this for a beat. It makes sense that Mike and Dustin don't *hate* basketball, but hate that it takes me away from them. Which is weird, since *they're* the ones who barely want to hang out these days. But they're slowly starting to get over it, which I think, as Robin says, will get better over time.

But none of this explains Max's reaction to my choices, and I tell Robin this. At the mention of Max, her eyebrows go up.

"Oh, that's a *very* different game there, Lucas."

"Why—because she's my girlfriend?"

"*Especially* because." She snaps her fingers. "Here's a little test for you: Who's the cause of the trouble you guys are having—you or her?"

I think on it. "Kinda . . . us both? Her, really, but—"

"Eeehhh!" Robin makes a buzzer sound, then shakes her head softly. "See, that's your first mistake in girlfriend-land. There's never a problem that's just one person's alone. Her problem is your problem, which means it's a *you both* problem. An *us* problem."

"I've tried everything," I say. "I don't think there's more I can do at this point to get her to open up to me, or even to make her feel better."

"Then maybe it's not about her opening up to you, or you making her feel better. Maybe it's just about you being there. Have you tried *being there,* Lucas?"

I squint. "I don't know . . . what that means. Or how I can *be there* if I'm not trying to help."

Robin leans forward. "Why don't you start by just being there, like, physically? Sit next to her and *listen.* Like, *really* listen. Don't speak, don't try to solve anything. Just . . . listen to what her silence is telling you."

Just sit and listen? It's the opposite of everything I am. One of my best skills is literally solving problems. I'm not sure how my relationship can be solved by me simply doing . . . nothing? But I don't want to sound ungrateful, so I tell Robin I'll think about it.

"And don't sweat all the other stuff. I see you wrote *Avoid relationship and friendship drama,* and I think that's great because you really don't want that to overshadow all the good times you can have, you know? Like, remember to live in the moment." She taps at my book. "You should add that to your list. After all, you only get to be in high school once. Don't spend your time putting out fires when you can enjoy the scenery." She points both thumbs at herself. "And if you ever need someone to bounce ideas off of . . ."

"Sure," I say, adding the new rule as she's suggested. "Let's hope I won't have to take you up on that."

With that, she returns to the counter. I'm almost out the door when she calls back to me.

"Forgot to tell you," she says. "We have the new one. Want me to ring that up right now?"

I glance around just like earlier, then say, "Sure."

She pulls the new tape out of the same private bag from before and slips it to me. I don't need to look at the full title to know it's the right one: *Pride and Passion: 1984 NBA Playoffs and Finals.*

"Thanks, Robin," I say. "I owe you."

"Don't sweat it," she says, then leans forward. "But if you really want some peace of mind? I'd say it's generally easier to be honest with friends."

It's weird to hear this from her, because insisting that other people always tell the truth used to be my stock-in-trade. To hear it directed at me is slightly uncomfortable.

"Okay," I say, then nod at the computer on the desk. "But until then, no records as usual, right?"

She gives me a thumbs-up. "You got it."

CHAPTER THIRTEEN

THURSDAY, NOVEMBER 28, 1985

Thanksgiving dinner at my house is one of the few times in the year that I get to spend the entire day with family. Before Uncle Jack and Dad reconnected, it used to be just us four. But in recent years, Uncle Jack hasn't missed a Thanksgiving dinner at our house, which means a table of five every year, and six whenever any of Dad's coworkers joins us. Mom used to advocate for smaller turkeys back in the day—she grew up on smaller Thanksgivings where quail was served. But after Uncle Jack became a regular, we switched to full turkeys. There are always enough leftovers.

Which works great, because the amount of food available today is of interest to me.

The house is bathed in a myriad of smells all day, and they've intensified by the time I come down the stairs for dinner. Turkey roast and stuffing aside, there's the smell of Mom's favorite corn bread. I peek into the kitchen, and beyond Mom's bustling, I can see the sources of the remaining smells: pecan pie, another one of her favorites; black beans, a delicacy she picked up from her mother; lemonade and sweet tea—also from her mother—and hard cider for the adults in the house.

Dad, Uncle Jack, and Erica are already at the table. Dad, who prefers to carve the turkey long before dinner, is already at work, flexing his two blades of choice. He likes to hold the turkey down with one long carving knife from the kitchen, and then cut through with his Gerber Mark II combat knife. It's a performance of dexterity, one that has drawn applause from Erica and me since we were kids. Even Uncle Jack, who often prefers to do all of the eating and none of the preparation, enjoys this part.

Tonight, my heart's not really in it as I watch Dad carve to Erica's and Uncle Jack's cheers. During the long shower I just took, all I could think about was why Max hadn't shown up to Family Video yesterday. Mike, Dustin, and I ended up having the movie night without her, but it was never about the movie night for me. It was about starting that road back to recovery with her.

In the note I left in her locker to meet us at Family Video, I'd also made sure to tell her she could come by my house for Thanksgiving dinner. Whatever's going on with her at home seems to be getting worse.

For instance, the clothes she's been wearing lately have been . . . unusual. Old and oversize, and not in a good way. They remind me of Will's clothes, how he was always wearing something of Jonathan's, or even Mrs. Byers's. I get the feeling that the Hargroves may not be doing so great moneywise. And with this being their first Thanksgiving without Billy, I suspect this year's Thanksgiving won't be their best.

Over the record player, "Fantasy" by Dad's favorite band, Earth Wind & Fire, plays softly. On the TV, which is turned down to zero volume, they're showing a rerun from earlier in the month of President Reagan accepting the Thanksgiving turkey at the White House. The turkey seems well-behaved, unlike last year's, which flapped away from the podium and strutted toward the press. Tonight, they're laughing, echoing the laughter at my own table, and probably at tables all over America. For once, everything seems so . . . normal.

But as Mom lays out the mashed potatoes, gravy, and cranberry sauce, I think about what Max is having for dinner tonight. Definitely not this. My gaze wanders to the door, and for a moment, I imagine that she's right about to walk in and join us just as I invited.

Soon, Dad is done with the carving, and Mom asks us to say grace. As everyone shuts their eyes, I take one last look at the door. No Max.

After our dinner prayer is over, I mumble an excuse to go use the bathroom. Then, when no one is looking, I veer toward the kitchen. Most of the food is on the table, but some meat and sides like stuffing, beans, mashed potatoes, and dessert are still in here. I pick out as much as I can, find a Tupperware that'll take them all, grab a jacket from the hallway, and sneak out of the house without a sound.

. . .

Elmore skatepark, at this time of night, is a concrete desert lit by overhead lamps. Doesn't help that tonight is the most family-oriented holiday in all of America. So when I spot Max, seated in her usual spot at the barrier on the edge of the park, it seems like even more of a sad picture.

I ride up to her slowly to keep from scaring her. I recognize her signature jeans, sneakers, and red hair tucked under a hoodie. Disheveled, but still pretty. I call out her name, but she can't hear me. Her ears are plugged with earphones connected to her Walkman. On the ground next to her is a cassette of Kate Bush's latest album, *Hounds of Love*. I can only make out the strains of the music, but I don't need to hear the words to know what she's listening to. "Running Up That Hill" is the first track of the A-side, so she always has it playing because it's the easiest to rewind to.

I stand there for a moment, watching her bob her head

to the music. Then, probably sensing my presence, she turns around slowly, then recoils.

"Jesus!" she says, pulling the earphones down. "Lucas?"

"Sorry, I was trying not to scare you."

"What're you doing here?" she says, hand on heart. "I thought you were at dinner?"

"I was," I say, "but I thought you could do with some holiday spirit." I stretch the Tupperware forward. "Happy Thanksgiving?"

She observes the container in my hand but makes no move to take it. "What's that?"

"Part of a Thanksgiving dinner," I say. "I decided if you weren't going to accept my invitation, then maybe I could bring Thanksgiving to you. Careful, though, it's my mom's good Tupperware, and I have to get it back tonight or I'm *dead*."

She eyes the container a bit more, then says, "No thanks."

"No thanks?"

"I don't need food, Lucas."

"It's not *food*, Max, it's Thanksgiving dinner."

"I don't want your family's leftovers, Lucas. I'm not a charity case."

This isn't charity, I want to say, but what's the point? She's already angry—anything I say to contradict her will just make things worse. So I drop down and sit on the barrier next to her.

"Max," I say. "I want to help you deal with . . . what you're dealing with. But I don't know how to because I don't *know* what's wrong. So . . . please, tell me what it is, and I'll do whatever I can to help make it better."

She shakes her head. "That's just the problem, Lucas. I'm not high school or Hawkins or your life. I don't need you to *fix* me."

Robin's words rush back to me. *Have you tried being there, Lucas? Listen to what her silence is telling you.*

I place the dinner on the concrete between us, then sigh.

"I'm sorry," I say. And then: "Can I . . . listen to some music with you?"

She's surprised by this change in demeanor. She creases her brow, unsure of what my game plan is. So I take the Walkman, which has been playing this whole time, and then push rewind. The tape whirs as it spins backward.

" 'Running Up That Hill' is your favorite, right?" I say. She nods.

The tape finishes whirring and clicks to a stop. I push the play button, crank the volume up to its highest, and set the Walkman down between us. The strains of the relentless drums and lead melody come on. Through the flat earphones, it sounds like a tin radio, but it's loud enough in the silent night, where the only contest for the Walkman is crickets.

Kate Bush begins to sing. I've never really listened to the song other than once when Max let me. But as I sit there and follow Robin's advice, I realize, suddenly, that she's singing about making a deal with God for her lover to swap places with her so he can feel her emotions without her having to explain it. She's singing about exchanging their experiences so they'd never be unhappy anymore.

She's singing about me and Max.

I look at Max, and there are tears in her eyes. She looks back at me, and I can tell she's realized the same thing I have.

Max mumbles something soft, her voice barely a whisper.

"What?"

She reaches forward and stops her Walkman. Silence envelops us again.

"I live in a trailer park," she says, a crack in her voice.

Just sit and listen.

"Neil left my mom," she says after a beat. "Left her with nothing. So now we live in Forest Hills, up east. That's why I'm here. Because we can't afford a turkey this year."

"I'm so sorry, Max."

A tear falls down her cheek. She wipes it with the back of her sleeve.

"It's not like I don't want to come to Thanksgiving dinner at your house, Lucas," she says. "Or to *Super Mario* in Mike's basement, or to movie nights, or to see *Godzilla*. It's just . . ." She pauses. "There's just too much . . . *change* in my life right now. I can't pretend that everything's normal."

She flips the hood of her jacket over her head. It's getting chilly.

"I want you to know—I understand what you're doing. I know you don't think I'm a charity case. I know you're bringing me dinner because you think I deserve to be happy, and you want to try to make me happy. But . . ." She sighs. "It's hard to look around and see everyone doing fine when everything in my life is going to shit. Nothing stays the same for long, and everyone—good or bad—leaves eventually. No matter how hard I try, nothing ever works out." She shrugs. "So what's the point of trying anymore?"

"Max . . ."

She looks up at me. "I don't know if I can ever be happy, Lucas. Not even with you."

She doesn't say it. She doesn't need to. Listening to the silence in that moment, I can finally hear loud and clear what she's been trying to tell me all this time.

I can't be with you anymore.

Max pushes the rewind button on the Walkman. The whirring fills the space between us, and then she pushes play. Once more, Kate Bush sings about her lover and the pain she wishes that he could understand.

Inside me, different dragons fight each other. The dragon of rage wants me to be angry, to remind her of all I've done and sacrificed just for her. To emphasize how hard I've tried to be a good boyfriend. Another dragon wants me to remember that Max is still my friend, that she's

going through a hard time, and maybe I need to understand that without my boyfriend ego getting in the way.

But the dragon of silence, which wants me to do nothing but listen, wins.

And so Max and I sit there together, listening to Kate
Bush sing. For the first time in our relationship, our breakup
feels final.

CHAPTER FOURTEEN

THURSDAY, NOVEMBER 28, 1985

Once I get home, I park my bike quietly. I figure that after wondering where I was for the rest of dinner, everyone's gone off to bed by now. So I do the only thing I think makes sense: climb up the pipe by the side of my bedroom window and get in as silently as possible.

It's neither easy nor something I do all that often. Dad has very strong feelings about the outside walls getting stained as a result of repeated climbing. He thinks dirt on the walls reflects poorly on us. Also, a lot of the wood on the outside walls is falling apart, and he is scared that one of us could easily slip. He's not wrong. This pipe is not the sturdiest, and I don't weigh the same as I did in middle school.

Either way, I get into my room safely enough and without tracking much mud onto the wall or pipe. I must have made a ton of noise coming up, though, because I've barely settled in and taken off my jacket when I hear footfalls and whispering down the stairs. I'm still trying to make sense of it when Dad suddenly bursts into the room, Uncle Jack behind him, Mom and Erica behind them both. Dad has his shotgun trained on me; Uncle Jack has a baseball bat at the ready. Mom and Erica both hold kitchen knives.

"It's me, it's me," I say, hands in the air.

"Jesus, Lucas!" says Mom as they all breathe sighs of relief, lowering their weapons. "Don't scare us like that!"

"What are you—" Dad starts, then looks at the open window. "Did you climb in?"

"Yes," I say. "Sorry."

"So, you disappeared in the middle of family dinner *and* climbed into the house," says Dad. "That's two offenses, son."

"I'm sorry," I say. "But I had to help Max."

"Your friend who was supposed to show up for dinner?" asks Mom. "Did something happen to her?"

"No," I say, then: "Kinda. Her parents broke up, and she didn't get to have a real Thanksgiving, so I went to hang out with her at the park."

Dad, Mom, and Uncle Jack look at one another. From the firmness of his jaw, Dad clearly has his sights set on punishment. But Mom's giving him her soft look, and Uncle Jack tends to side with Mom more than with Dad.

Luckily for me, Mom's gaze wins out. Carefully, Dad gives Uncle Jack his shotgun to put away with the baseball bat, and Mom does the same with the kitchen knives, handing them to Erica.

Mom comes over and rubs my shoulder, mouthing a silent *sorry* in my direction and asking if I'm all right. Dad's eyes are busy roving all over the room. His gaze finally lands on my reading table.

"What's this?" he asks, picking up the book he has noticed and scanning the title.

Oh, shit. I was reading that right before taking a shower earlier and completely forgot to tuck it back under my bed. Just my luck. The *one* time Dad comes to my room in how long, he doesn't find a porn magazine or anything like that—no. Instead, he finds the *one* thing I didn't want him to see: Jay's book.

"*A History of the Negro in America,*" Dad says, reading the title aloud, then lifts it up. "Where did you get this?"

"Nowhere." I'm not about to get Jay into trouble.

"What d'you mean *nowhere*?" Dad insists. "Did Jack give you this?"

He turns to Mom. "If Jack gave him this, Susie, I swear to God—"

"I don't think Jack would give him anything without your permission, Charles," says Mom, then looks at me. "Right?"

I nod.

Dad looks at me, then at the book, then back at me.

"What's going on with you, Lucas? What are you trying to do to your life by trying to become some kind of radical?"

I frown. "Radical? I'm not—"

"Because that's what books like this are good for," he says. "Making Black people everywhere think that they have to become troublemakers to get ahead in this country. Is that what you want?"

"What do you mean *troublemaker?*" The question comes before I can second-guess myself.

"Excuse me?" Dad asks.

"I'm not—I—" I take a deep breath. "I don't think understanding ourselves and our history and where we come from is the same thing as being a troublemaker, Dad."

"Then you want to explain why they always out there making trouble?" Dad fires back. "Those folks in Philadelphia you run your mouth about—you want to tell me why, of all the Black people in Philly, they're the only ones that get targeted? The government doesn't just drop a bomb on *anyone,* Lucas." He slaps the book on the table. "It's people like this they target. And you know how people get to be like this? With books like *these.*"

I want to say the government has done worse things than drop a bomb, even down here in his beloved Hawkins, but Dad's not finished.

"I say it all the time—this is the problem with people like your Uncle Jack and many others in this country," he says. "They have this idea stuck in their heads that they belong to some royal court in some great *motherland*. Instead of putting their heads down, working hard like everyone else, and making this a safe place for their families like we've done here in Hawkins, they scream and scream and make themselves targets. They put their families in danger."

Dad's voice booms into the night, and his breathing is audible. I've never seen Dad so worked up. He's always the calm one in the house, preferring grunts and charged silence to raising his voice. This takes me by surprise.

"Charles, honey," Mom is saying. "It's late. Maybe we should talk about this tomorrow."

"No, we will finish this *tonight*," says Dad. He points to the book. "I don't want to see anything like this in this house again—book, tape, whatever. If I do, I'll burn it myself."

My mouth skitters ahead of my brain. "Maybe I won't have to read this book if we ever talk about these things at home."

Dad is already turning to go, but he stops at the threshold between the hallway and my bedroom.

"It's like a taboo to say the word *Black* in this house." The words carry more snap and bite than I intend. "Do you want me to keep pretending we're the same as everyone else? That *I'm* the same? Because I can't anymore." I point at the book. "I'll return the book if you want, but I wouldn't have been reading it in the first place if we'd just stop pretending we're white."

Silence hangs between us like a suspended crane. Dad does not looked at me. Mom is caught in the middle, casting glances each way.

"You know what the greatest lesson I learned in the military is, son?" Dad asks, breaking the silence. His eyes are fixed on a spot on the wall, so I'm not sure if he's talking to me. I shake my head anyway.

"A target is an enemy because someone has classified them so—that's something they cannot change, whether they like it or not. Such a target must make themselves smaller, not bigger, to survive." He pauses. "Do you understand what I'm saying, Lucas?"

A part of me wants to challenge him, wants to say: *Are you asking me to be small forever?* But there's something about when Dad speaks in that soft tone, the one with which he acknowledges that he's wrong, but is too proud to actually apologize. It tells me he knows why I'm reading this book. He understands that I need to read it to learn things for myself, but at the same time, he's too scared to witness me do exactly that.

"Yes," I say.

"That's all I want, son," he says, finally. "For you to be less of a target."

When he leaves, I sit in bed, pissed. *No end to this horrible day, is there?*

Mom doesn't leave with Dad. Instead, she sits next to me and sighs. For a while, neither of us speaks.

"Why does he hate being Black?" I ask, breaking the silence.

She sighs again. "You know why your father calls me Susie instead of Sue, like everyone else?"

I shake my head.

"That's what I used to be called. I was always Susie—to my family, to my friends. My *Black* family and friends. Until I got into the world, and suddenly, I was Sue."

I squint. "I don't understand."

"Well, apparently, the name *Sue Sinclair* makes everyone think I'm a white woman until they meet me. That name, on paper, can get me through doors that might otherwise hesitate to let in . . ." She gestures at herself, her skin. *"Susie."*

"Oh."

"Yeah. But your dad, he's never been a fan of that name, Sue. So he's the only one left—especially here in Hawkins—who calls me Susie, like I'm still the girl he knew before all of this. In a way, it's become like our special little thing."

I nod.

"Your father doesn't hate being Black, Lucas," she says. "He's just . . . tired of what being Black means in a white world."

"He should try being the *one* Black nerd in all of Hawkins High."

Mom shifts in her seat to face me. "Look, I know it's

hard for you, that there are things we don't discuss in this house." She massages my shoulder. "But I can promise you it's only because we—your dad and I—are trying our best to protect you. We're learning how to raise you in this world, but we're not perfect. We're still learning to live in it, too."

"By keeping me in the dark about who I am? About my history?"

"We're not keeping you in the dark, no. We're choosing not to burden you. That's all we have. For now, at least."

"But I *am* burdened, whether you like it or not. I'm still Black every day I step out into this same world you're describing."

She's lost in thought, but finally accedes.

"I agree," she says. "And I agree that you should learn what it means to be a young Black man in this town, in this country, in this world. But I don't want you listening to just anyone, or gaining that understanding from just anybody. So if I were you, I'd return the book as your dad has said."

I start to protest, but she holds up a finger. "Ah—*but*—that doesn't mean you can't get the stories you want elsewhere. You'll just have to do it with someone your dad will approve of."

"Like who?"

She shrugs. "There are people better suited to orienting you with Black life in Hawkins. There's Chief Powell, who's pretty much seen everything. There's good ol' Eugene at the farmers' market. I could call the McKinneys—their son Patrick's also on the basketball team, I hear. Maybe you can talk to him?"

I want to tell her that finding Black people to talk to me is not going to solve the problem. Besides, I already have that in Jay. What I need is to know that there's someone I can talk to when the going gets tough, someone who'll listen to me without judgment. Lucky for me, that's *also* Jay, who I'll see at practice over the weekend.

So I just nod because it's late and I've had a bad day and I want to go to sleep. Mom takes this as her cue to leave, kisses my forehead, and heads back to her room. I shut the door and fall into bed.

CHAPTER FIFTEEN

"Triple threat! Right foot—quick stop! Okay, now jog to half-court."

It's the weekend, and Jay and I are at our last practice before JV trials. He's taking me through a rehash of footwork drills first, because according to him, even though these will be the least important part of tryouts, they'll matter most during games. Performing well during games, he says, is what moves players from the JV squad to the varsity bench and finally to the starting team.

Today, he's dressed in a lean scrimmage vest over a gray practice T-shirt that says *Tiger Pride*. We're at the nearest neighborhood court, a number of streets off Maple. Not close enough to my house for me to know any of the people who come by to play, but not so far that Mom won't let me bike there alone. Jay, on the other hand, has to come all the way over from across the railway tracks, where he lives.

We do suicide drills next.

"Why do we call them suicides again?" I ask, panting from the run.

"'Cause you work yourself breathless?" he says, then angles his head. "Yeah, now that you mention it, kinda sounds like a poor choice of words."

"Yup."

"Maybe we stick with *line drills* going forward?"

"Good call."

"All right. Race you to full court?"

After that, we get into ballhandling, his commands ringing in my ears as I try to follow them while sweat drips all over me. He takes me through passing ("Feet on the floor! No bullets, no rainbows!"), catching ("Hands, eyes, feet—you catch with all three"), and dribbling ("Eyes on the court, eyes on the court!").

Somewhere between the warm sun on my shoulders, the squeak of sneakers on hard court, and the feel of rubber in my hands, I forget about jocks and jackets and the promise of cool. I forget the niggling feeling that I'm being shunted toward this sport because, apparently, Black boys everywhere are simply expected to play it. I forget, and am delighted to admit that *basketball is fun!* Hanging out and playing with Jay gives me the same warm fuzzies I get playing D&D. Pity Mike and Dustin may never know this joy. How cool would it be if all four of us were here right now, playing, laughing, living our best lives?

We leave shooting for last, as that's my weakest point. I've labored over my shooting, but for some reason, I can't seem to make any headway with it. At a point, I get so frustrated that Jay is forced to step in and ask me to take a chill pill.

"It's okay to have weaknesses," he says. "Just make sure your strong points are good. That kinda averages you out, but that's okay. We don't have to be our best all the time."

"I just want to be good," I say.

"No," he says. "You only have to be *enough* for yourself. Everything else is secondary."

He takes me through something he calls the BEEF system—balance ("Feet apart and staggered, Sinclair!"), elbows in ("Ninety degrees to the ground, Lucas!"), eyes on the rim ("Aim for the middle hook!"), and follow through ("Always snap your wrist!"). We stay on this section of practice for the better part of an hour.

Jay's not a hard-liner, but he's firm, insistent. When he needs to, he grabs the ball from me and demonstrates the moves he wants me to get better at. And boy, doesn't he get them all right! From shooting to dribbling to passing, his skills are all silky smooth, top-notch.

"Why aren't you on the starting team again?" I ask, when we take five to rehydrate at the benches before our last training hour of the day.

"Again, as I've said, I'm a three, a small forward. You know who else is a small forward?"

"Jason," I say. "Right. Can't displace the captain."

"Exactly. I could play as a four, or even a two. But those are Patrick's and Andy's spots, and those guys have been playing with Jason since, like, they were all toddlers. Their chemistry is insane. No sensible coach will bench any one of them unless they're injured. And, of course, I can't play as a center because I'm not big enough. So, as much as I want to play, I completely understand Coach benching me."

"What about point guard? I feel like you could give Charlie a run for his money."

Jay laughs. "Why don't *you* give Charlie a run for his money? You're the one who's a bona fide point guard."

"Bona fide is stretching it," I say. "I haven't even passed tryouts yet."

"Nah, making JV is easy," he says. "The real test is jumping from JV to varsity, even as a sub. You have to prove yourself." He looks at me. "Sorry, again, that I can't be there. I've got this makeup biology test and I really need to ace it."

"Nah, don't sweat it."

"You'll do fine. Plus, it's not like you're dead set on the team or anything. You're just trying something new, right?"

"Right."

"Then just plan to have fun."

We're preparing to get back onto the court when a new group of older boys—young men, really, probably college students home for the holidays—enter the court. They set up at both hoops, leaving us with no practice space left. I'm about to inform them that we were here first and therefore the current occupiers of one rim, but Jay holds me back.

"No need," he says, watching the boys shoot us dagger gazes.

"Why?"

"Let's call it a day."

"We still have—"

"Lucas," he says gently. "Look at these guys."

There's twelve of them, all white boys. They don't speak to us but continue to scowl, daring us to come ask for our rim back.

"This is their neighborhood," says Jay. "Let them have it."

I clench my fist by my side, ready to press the matter, but Jay puts a hand on my shoulder.

"How about some ice cream," he says, "to cool off?"

...

The Fair Mart is empty because it's the weekend after Thanksgiving and most people are still caught up in the holiday spirit, spending time indoors with family. Lucky for us, packaged ice cream is half off and not yet sold out.

We each get a squeezable new Soft Swirl—me raspberry, Jay chocolate—and find a nearby bench. It's definitely too cold for us to be eating ice cream outside without jackets on, but I'd rather do this than be stuck at home with Erica, or with Mopey Mike or Never-Ending Dustin.

"Back there," I say. "Why did you ask me not to confront them?"

Jay chuckles. "What were you going to do—take on twelve college guys all on your own?"

"I wasn't going to *fight*," I say. "Just wanted to tell them that we were there first."

"Well," says Jay, shrugging, "it's their court, so they can do whatever they want."

"Not, it's not," I say. "It's a public court."

Jay shakes his head. "Lucas, Lucas, Lucas. Open your eyes. The sign may say *public* on it, but it's always been theirs. Everything always is." He leans forward. "You been reading that book I lent you?"

"Yeah," I say, reaching into my bag to pull it out. "But only just the first chapter, which is too bad because I have to return it."

"Why?"

"My dad," I say without further explanation. "Maybe if you have something else that's not so conspicuous?"

For some reason, Jay doesn't press further. He just nods, accepts the book, and tucks it into his backpack. Then he pulls out something else: *Harper's Magazine*. It's got a red cover with an illustration of an icy mountain with green trees and little snow-capped houses. Looks like somewhere in Europe. An old edition, too, judging by how weather-beaten it is. I peer closer. *October 1953*. So *old* old, then.

Jay points to the lower right corner. "Ever heard of this guy, James Baldwin?"

"James who?"

"He's a phenomenal writer. One of the best out there. This essay, 'Stranger in the Village,' it's about this tiny village he visits in Switzerland and how the people are so excited to see a Black man like him for the first time. He talks about feeling like a stranger there, but that it's not any different from here in America, where he also feels like a stranger every day for being a Black man living in a country designed for white people." He thrusts the magazine at me. "You should read it for yourself. At least this one your dad won't ask you to return because he'll never know."

I accept the magazine sheepishly. "Thanks."

"Don't sweat it," he says, then pauses. "I'm still surprised. You said history's your favorite subject at school, so I thought you'd know Baldwin."

"I know MLK and Malcolm X and the like."

"Even white people know King and Malcolm." He squints at me, suddenly all serious. "It's more like—what are your connections to your Black self, you know? Not that you must know *everything* and *everyone,* but more like— who and what are your own touchstones?"

I've never really thought about it that way. Growing up, Mom and Dad never taught us to think of anything as *white people stuff* versus *Black people stuff*. Nothing has ever felt off-limits to me. Movies, games, music—I don't care where it comes from as long as I like it.

But a part of me sees Jay's point. I consider the way Dad switches stations immediately when that rapper, LL Cool J, comes on. Or how he says Eddie Murphy is too crass for us. Erica secretly watches him sometimes—it's where she gets all her swear words. Maybe I just haven't been paying attention. Somehow, I've unintentionally been doing exactly what Dad wants, steering myself away from all the stuff with Black people in it. Maybe he set a big trap and I fell into it.

Well, now I know better. If I'm going to live in this world as a Black boy, it's just normal that I'll end up enjoying some stuff that other Black people do.

"Okay, let's try this," I say. "Name all the Black stars you know, and I'll see who I know."

He begins to mention names. Some, like Michael Jackson, I do know—the "Thriller" video was on nonstop throughout last Halloween. Magic Johnson, Michael Jordan—now that I've gotten into basketball and watched so many tapes. Mr. T from *Rocky*. Tina Turner, Prince—Mom and Dad are big fans and have vinyl records of them at home.

But some others, I've only heard vague mentions of in passing, or have heard nothing about at all. Whoopi Goldberg. Cicely Tyson. Some dude called Kurtis Blow.

"Look, I'm gonna play something for you." He pulls out his Walkman and earphones from his backpack, followed by a cassette with two guys on the cover, but only their hats are visible. The words *Run-D.M.C.* and *King of Rock* are highlighted above their heads.

He hands me the earphones, fast-forwards the tape, then pushes play.

Two dudes start rapping, just like LL Cool J and the others do. But then, out of nowhere, guitar power chords come in, riffing along with the drumbeat. Both jam in sync, playing off of each other, while the rappers continue over the beat. In perfect unison. Just like many things I've learned since meeting Jay, it's a mixture of things I've, for some reason, always believed have no business being together. But here it is—drumbeats and guitar, rap and rock, "Black music" and "white music"—coexisting.

I pull off the headphones. "How do you do it?"

"Do what?"

"Mix everything together?"

He frowns, confused. "I didn't do that—Run-D.M.C. did."

"No, no," I say, laughing. "I mean, you . . . always find a way to be everything you want to at once."

"Hmm." He puts a hand on his lip, pondering it. "I guess . . . I try to remind myself that it's okay to be more than one thing at once, you know? Even if when you put it all together, it doesn't make sense to the world. I can be a jock, but I still like to read Baldwin." He puts on a voice like a TV announcer. *"Do I contradict myself? Very well then I contradict myself. I am large, I contain multitudes."*

I laugh. "What in God's name does that mean?"

"It's Walt Whitman. The poet? 'Song of Myself'?"

I shake my head. "That's more like something my friend Dustin would know." I squint. "Now see, that's one of the weird things—that you know . . . poetry."

Jay cocks his head. "Like I said, I contain multitudes. And so does everyone, if they'll just let every part of who they are shine."

I get back to listening to Run-D.M.C. When the tape ends, he flips it around and plays me a song on the B side: "Can You Rock It Like This." I listen to it until our ice creams are gone.

Afterward, we pack up and walk our bikes. He makes sure to walk me to our intersection—yet another of Mom's requirements for going out alone.

"So, a breakup, huh?" says Jay once we're on our way.

I've been having such a great day that I completely forgot I told him about my breakup with Max. He didn't say anything at the time because we got into practice right after. I thought he didn't care or that he forgot. Seems he'd just been waiting for an opportunity to ask.

"Yeah," I say. "Don't wanna think about it much. As you said—*avoid relationship drama*."

"Well . . ." He tilts his head. "When I said that, I didn't mean don't *think* about it. I just said don't let it consume your life. A breakup is a big deal—they're hard. But I get it if you don't want to talk about it. . . ." He pauses. "You doing all right, at least?"

Honestly, I haven't asked myself that question yet. Maybe because the truth is that I don't know. Some part of me feels like I'm supposed to feel guilty, that I must have somehow failed Max for her to break up with me. But some other part of me is at peace with it, because I understand that she needs space to find herself. Who am I to get in the way of that? Neither of these options make me any less sad, though.

"I kinda miss her," I say. "Every day. But I'm not sure I want to tell her that." I look up. "Does that make sense?"

"Feelings don't need to make sense, Lucas."

"Yeah," I say. "I just think it's best for both of us. For now."

Jay nods, and we don't say anything else until we get to my intersection. I make a mental note of how he's doing the exact thing I was supposed to be doing with Max all along: listening.

Once at the intersection, he veers off on his own route, throwing me a thumbs-up.

"Good luck Monday, dude," he says. "Give them everything."

CHAPTER SIXTEEN

MONDAY, DECEMBER 2, 1985

"Ball!" screams Mr. Theo, assistant coach of the Hawkins Tigers junior varsity team.

A basketball whizzes through the air toward a freshman, one of only three trying out for the team. He flinches as it arrives, anticipating the hit but pushing his arms forward anyway. The ball lands in his hands, and he grips. Not a bad catch either. But that first flinch is a deal breaker. And it turns out Mr. Theo hates flinches more than anything.

"You're out!" screams Mr. Theo, closing in on the freshman. "There's no place for fear on this team, you hear me? No place!"

The boy who threw the ball—a junior from the varsity

subs roster—snickers. His boys, who've come by to watch and be overall jackasses, laugh as well.

JV tryouts are off to a not-so-great start.

I completely forgot that PE is the first period of the week. Apparently, some random study convinced the school board that increasing heart rate before school helps with brain oxygen and information retention. What the person in charge of that study did not account for, of course, is the funk that comes from not being able to shower before going to class. Not only is the experience uncomfortable, but it's a death sentence for all noses for the rest of the day. Also, some people—like me—get nervous if we don't get enough prep time before physical activities.

My hands are shaking. They shouldn't be, because I already gave myself a pep talk, repeating what Jay said. *Just enjoy yourself.* But it's hard to do that with all this screaming going on.

Mr. Theo blows on his whistle. He's a lanky man in a gray T-shirt and shorts that ride up his thighs. Much younger than most teachers and the head coach, but no less strict. The veins on his neck pop, so he always looks like he's about to fight someone. Except, he doesn't look scary at all, no matter how hard he tries. He just looks like a nice man who's stressed.

"You," Mr. Theo says, pointing to the freshman beside me. "You're next."

This new dude is taller than me, and the set of his freckled face tells me he might be someone who knows what he's doing. Also, his shoes. He's not wearing ordinary gym shoes like I am, but proper basketball sneakers. The kind I've seen the pros wear on the NBA tapes. And they're scuffed, too, so they have definitely been played in.

He aligns his body in preparation, feet forward, elbows angled. This kid is confident, like this is second nature.

"Ball," Mr. Theo says. The junior thumps the ball at the freshman. The boy catches it, hard and firm.

"Again," says Mr. Theo. The ball is returned and the junior fizzes another bullet pass. The freshman catches it again.

"Good," says Mr. Theo. "Now lemme see your dribbling and scoring form."

The freckled boy bounces the ball and glides forward, his movement smooth and confident. It's so obvious he's been playing for a while that even the upperclassmen don't laugh, but instead watch, enraptured. This is clearly someone who's competing for space on that varsity roster.

The boy steps forward, lifts off one foot, taps the ball against the board. Net.

"All right, now lemme see you shoot a two-pointer," says Mr. Theo.

The boy retrieves the ball, shoots from inside the D, scores. Mr. Theo then asks him for a three-pointer from outside the D. I can hear a collective draw of sharp breath from the upperclassmen, but the freshman boy doesn't flinch. He steps outside the D, bounces, takes the shot. Misses. The upperclassmen holler. But the freshman retrieves the ball, tries again, and this time, he scores.

Finally, Mr. Theo asks him for a couple of free throws, which he nets easily.

"All right," says Mr. Theo. "Seems you know what you're doing, young man. What's your name?"

"Lee Garroway," says the freckled boy.

"You're in, Garroway," says Mr. Theo. "Practice is same time next week. Miss the first day, and you're out." Then he turns toward me. "Next!"

I clench my fists as I step up to the center circle. Despite all the practice sessions and NBA tapes, there's no way I'm anything close to what Garroway has demonstrated here.

"Ball!" screams Mr. Theo. I swallow and brace myself.

The ball zooms toward me. I brace, prepare my arms, keep my feet firm as Jay taught me.

It's an easy catch.

"Again," says Mr. Theo. I toss the ball back to the junior, but the pass is short. The ball bounces, then rolls toward him. The boys in the bleachers snicker.

"That how you pass"—he consults the sign-up sheet—"Sinclair?"

"No, sir."

"Better keep that kinda pass out of my court. Ball!"

The ball comes at me, fast and without warning. Before I have time to think about positioning or steadying myself, it whacks me in the shoulder. I find myself one knee down on the court, massaging my shoulder. The laughter of the upperclassmen rings in my ears.

"No aloofness in my court, young man," says Mr. Theo. "Get up!"

I rise gingerly. I don't hear Mr. Theo's third cry for *Ball!* but I know it's coming, so I brace and plant my feet. It's a fast pass, but I catch it quite well.

"Now, lemme see you dribble and score," says Mr. Theo.

I do my best. I'm not sure dribbling is my strong suit. I find I'm much better at taking the ball off Jay—guarding, anticipating, lunging at the right moment. But dribbling with no opponent is easy, so I move just enough to get to the paint and toss a jump shot into the net.

"All right, gimme a two- and three-pointer," says Mr. Theo.

Two-pointer is easy. This is pretty much what a lot of my shooting practice with Jay was, as well as shooting practice with the new hoop Dad installed in the driveway.

My three-pointer is a complete failure. I get five tries, and I score none. The upperclassmen holler. Mr. Theo shakes his head.

"At least tell me you're better at free throws?" He points me toward the free throw line.

I take the ball and shoot another five times. Two in, three misses. One of them goes straight to board and doesn't even hit the rim at all.

"Why did you sign up for this?" Mr. Theo says, shaking his head as I pant, sweat dripping down my forehead. He writes a few notes on his clipboard, shakes his head some more, then says, "Lucas, is it?"

"Yes, sir."

"Yeah, I'll have to think on this one. Feeder team might be short, but so help me God, I'd rather be short than burdened with stupid." He waves his hand. "Off you go."

I drag my bag and shuttle out of the gym. It takes me a moment to realize I can't return to class like this. But I also can't use the changing room and showers, since that's what the team uses. So instead, I find myself in a bathroom stall, swapping sweaty shirt for hoodie and trying not to cry.

■ ■ ■

The rest of the school day is a wreck. As predicted, everyone smells like wet socks. I can't wait until it's lunch period to jump out of class and breathe. But once the bell rings and I'm out of there, the hallway's no better—it's just more post-PE people. I zigzag through them, trying to get to my next class and stick my head out a window.

There are people crowded around the notice board, which is strange because, at this time of year, most extracurricular groups have already announced their sign-up lists. Most, except . . .

Oh, shit.

I run down the hall to the board. I expected Mr. Theo to take a day or two deciding on additions to the JV squad, not a few hours.

Sure enough, the notice is titled: *Hawkins Tigers: Final Roster for '85–86 Basketball Season.* At the top are the five starters—Jason, Patrick, Andy, Charlie, Noah. Below that, subs—I spot Jermaine Demario in there.

Below those, on a fresh sheet, is written *Junior Varsity Roster.* It lists all the sophomores who didn't make it onto the first-team subs last year. But below that, two new names have been added: *Lee Garroway* and *Lucas Sinclair.*

I pump a fist in silent celebration. *I got in!*

The tall, freckled Garroway boy walks by the board with some friends. He doesn't stop by to look if his name's up—which is fair, because Mr. Theo already told him he's in. But then he clocks me looking at the board and pumping my fist, and does the math.

I give him a thumbs-up to say, *Hey, we made it!* But he just looks at me for a long time, then shakes his head, turning to his friends.

"Coach Theo thinks every Black person who can hold a ball is Magic Johnson," Lee says. "Even when they're absolute shit."

It's a whisper, with his back to me, but I hear it, clear as day. Their laughter rings in my ears as they walk away.

Monsters. Max's voice, from the cinema. *Even when they don't look like monsters.*

I watch Lee and his friends go. Part of me wants to walk up to him, to say, *Hey, say that to my face!* But the other part of me is thinking: *Is he right?* Jason did say the same thing. Do they all assume I'm only trying out for the team *because*

I'm Black—because I'm *supposed* to? Then I turn the question to myself: *Did I do this because they expect me to?* I think back to the warm fuzzies I get during training with Jay and decide: *No.* Basketball *is* fun. I want to play it because it gives me room to be something different. And I like being something different.

The only question I'm left with is the same one I asked on that first day, the only one I still can't answer: *But did I only get in because I'm Black?*

I'm not so sure I even want to know the answer. At least I get something good out of who I am. That, on its own, is enough.

CHAPTER SEVENTEEN

Since I made the team, we've had exactly one practice session, and it did not go well. Not for me, at least. Nothing prepared me for the chaos of actual drills—not the hours of tape I watched or number of driveway practices I ran on my own. Everyone but me seemed to know what they were doing. Mr. Theo would give a command, and they'd immediately know what it meant and how to respond. I was left standing too many times, unsure of what I was supposed to do, or taking a second or two longer to understand the command. And sure, Jay did scream during our practice sessions, but never as loud as Mr. Theo. His commands are thunderous when directed at me.

When I arrive at PE on Monday, Mr. Theo divides us into two teams—skins and shirts. He splits us two freshmen between the two sides, which are already made up of mostly sophomores. Lee Garroway ends up in skins, and I end up on the shirts side, which is great because I hate showing my bare chest in public. But it soon becomes clear that the shirts side doesn't want me. They grumble when it's announced I'm on their side, and I'm sure they would've asked me to sit on the bench if we weren't exactly five.

Worse, it turns out a couple people have skipped their own PE periods to hang out in the gym and are suddenly interested in the practice game. *A couple* is how my eyes count them, but in my mind, they feel like so much more. Especially when, out of nowhere, Mike and Dustin show up with . . . Erica?

My eyes widen as all three of them sit on the front benches in the practice court.

"What are you doing here?" I ask, hurrying over to them. To Erica: "What are *you* doing here. You're supposed to be at school!"

"And miss watching you flap at a ball like a fish out of water?" She scoffs. "Besides, you know school security is so full of holes, it's literally a basket."

"*She* told us you were playing," says Dustin. He and Mike are still dressed in their gym shirts, so they're clearly skipping like everyone else.

"We thought: What the hell?" says Mike. "Let's go cheer our friend or something."

"No, no cheering," I say, glancing over my shoulder at my team, who start flashing me looks for leaving in the middle of a huddle. "Listen, guys, I really appreciate you coming out to watch me play and all, but this is . . . maybe not the game to do it?"

"Why not?" asks Mike.

"Because it's . . . boring. It's not a *real* game."

"Looks real enough to me," he says. "Wait—are you *scared*?"

"Me, scared? Of what?"

"That we're going to watch you play like shit," says Erica. "One of your teammates—I dunno which one—he has a sister in my class. She's always yapping on about how he's going to show his skills and make the starting team." She cocks her head. "You don't think you're going to *lose* to him, are you?"

"Okay, first, Erica, *language*. Also, I dunno what you're talking about. I'm just surprised—I wasn't expecting you guys."

"Well, then, *surprise*," says Dustin, crossing his legs. "Just pretend we're not here." He nudges me back onto the court. "Look, look, they're calling you. Go."

As I jog back to the team, shaking my head, he yells: "Break a leg!"

This will not end well.

At the whistle, the skins team attacks us with ferocity, zipping passes so fast I can barely keep track. I try to stick to my job: steals, dropping deep to retrieve the ball, and starting fast breaks. But every time I get close to someone, they bundle me over. Worse, Mr. Theo won't blow for a foul, just tells me to get up and keep it moving. Soon my teammates begin to do the same, calling me a feather ("The wind blows and you fall, Sinclair!"). From the benches, it seems like except Mike and Dustin, everyone's laughing too, including Erica, who's totally having the time of her life.

Shirts lose to skins. Badly.

Mr. Theo rounds us up after.

"I hope you learned a good lesson today, which is that a team's only as strong as its weakest link." He points to me. "Looking at you, Sinclair." He returns to the group.

"If you ever want to make it to varsity, you can never—and I mean *never*—be the weakest link down here in JV. 'Cause then you'll go out there and be the weakest link for the Tigers, too, and we can't have that. Anyone who costs the Tigers a game doesn't just cost Coach a game. You're costing your teammates, your friends, your neighbors, this school, this town—you're taking us all down with you. Remember that."

Mr. Theo's words settle on me as I pack up my stuff, dejected. Maybe joining the basketball team wasn't such a great idea after all. The weight of expectations, the fact that all these people expect me to have inborn basketball talent—that's not what I came here for. I'm not here to carry the Tigers on my back. I just want to try something new.

I don't go back to the rest of the team to tell them anything, or to say *good game*. I just meet up with my friends by the benches.

"Good game," says Mike, patting me on the back like a teammate.

"Yeah," Dustin concurs, doing the same. "I didn't know you could play like that. Like—you even scored a shot."

"You know they lost, right?" says Erica. "Did we watch the same game? He scored *one* free throw—of four. Zero jump shots and no layups scored. He's literally the reason they lost."

Dustin shoots Erica a look to stop talking, but it's pointless because Erica listens to nobody. Also, she's right. I did cost my team the game.

The rest of the sophomores on the skins team walk past me as they track out of the gym. Lee Garroway, who scored a bunch of their points, is in the middle of them, getting all the praise. He clocks me, then whispers to one of the other sophomores. I get a quick flashback to the jocks whispering to one another before pulling Dustin's hair in the cafeteria on our first day.

Before I know what's happening, the boy Lee was whispering to leans forward as they walk past us and says to me: "Oreo."

I do a double take, unsure if I heard that right. *Did he just . . . ?*

They're all laughing, walking away. I'm too shocked at the brazenness to respond.

"Hey!" Erica says, stepping in front of me. "You better watch your mouth, dipshit. Nobody talks to my brother like that."

"What a bunch of jerks," says Dustin, shaking his head. "I dunno how you manage to be in the presence of these idiots all the time."

"How do they think calling you a cookie's an insult?" asks Mike. "They think you're soft? Who wouldn't fall down if someone pushed them like that?"

Mike and Dustin keep on talking, but the sound of their voices filters out. I shoot Erica a glance, and she shoots me one back. *They don't get it.*

For a moment, I think she's going to say the quiet part out loud, as she usually does, and harass Mike and Dustin for being so dumb. But she doesn't say anything, just stares at the retreating boys.

I remember, now, that she's also been called this name. She gets the gravity of it as much as I do. Mom once explained it to us. *Black on the outside, white on the inside.*

"Let's get out of here," I say, shepherding Mike and Dustin forward. To Erica, I point in the opposite direction. "Back to school *now,* or I'm telling Dad."

She scoffs, rolls her eyes, and is about to pull out one of her usual comebacks but stops short. She looks at me for a while, then says: "Those boys are jerks. And you're not *that* shit."

After she leaves, Mike and Dustin walk me down to

homeroom. All the while, they talk about their new Hellfire campaign, and how the Hellfire Club didn't get many new sign-ups this year because people think it's some sort of satanic cult. Apparently, the media reports have been leaning into the narrative about Hawkins being cursed by the devil. Not only Hawkins—people all over the country have apparently started to believe that there are demonic forces spreading across the country, just like Mom.

I half listen as they talk, but my mind is still on the basketball court. I can't stop thinking about all of my mistakes, being the weakest link, an Oreo. When I wanted to try out for basketball, I never expected being Black to factor into it. They said I got on the team because I was Black. Barely a week later, in a sick twist of irony, I'm now shit at basketball—because I'm not . . . Black enough?

Jay was right. There's no winning with this. And if there's no winning, then maybe there's no point.

At the door to Mr. Lansdale's class, I turn to my friends.

"Guys, I think . . . I need a break from basketball."

They stop short and look at each other, then back at me.

"You sure about that?" asks Dustin.

"You worked really hard," says Mike. "Practiced *all the time.*"

"I know," I say. "But I just . . . can't. It's just too much right now."

They look at each other again, then Dustin places a hand on my shoulder.

"Okay, well, how about something to take your mind off it?" he says. "We still have low enrollment down at Hellfire, right, Mike?"

"Right," says Mike.

"I know Eddie's all proud and saying no new additions until the semester ends, but I can talk to him. We'll sub you in for one game, he'll see how awesome you are at D&D, and he'll have to let you in. Some D&D, and you can forget basketball for a while. Sound good?"

I'm not sure I'm ready to *quit* quit just yet. It's only the first practice, right? But a huge part of me knows I won't be hurrying back to that court anytime soon. Subbing into one fun D&D game is not the worst idea.

"Deal," I say.

CHAPTER EIGHTEEN

THURSDAY, DECEMBER 19, 1985

I manage to avoid Jay for two whole days before he finds me.

By now word has gotten around, within ninth grade and beyond, that I'm no good at basketball. The sophomores on the JV team told those on the varsity subs roster, who then shared this info with their pals in subs. I'm pretty sure the starting upperclassmen are aware now, and possibly Coach as well. I'm *definitely* sure Jay knows, which is why I'd been hiding from him. I was hoping to hold out for the rest of the week and go into the holiday season without having to explain what happened at the JV practice game.

No such luck, though.

On Thursday morning, I'm about to stuff my books

into my locker and head for my first period when I spot Jay, walking toward me from his locker in the sophomore section down the hallway. No, *storming* toward me. He wears a deep frown and looks mighty upset, an expression I haven't yet seen him have, and it scares me.

It takes me a moment to process that he's covered in glitter.

The stuff is everywhere—plastered onto his face with sweat; sprinkled all over his striking hair; spattered over the front of his shirt. There's no part of his body it hasn't touched—eyelids, chin, elbow, jeans, sneakers. People giggle as he walks past them, but he pays no attention.

"What—" I start to say as he approaches me.

"Don't touch that locker," he says.

"What?"

"Don't open that." His voice is stern in a way I've never heard. His tone reminds me of the way Mike sometimes tells Holly not to get out of her chair. Like an older brother.

"Your combination?" says Jay, his finger poised over lock. I give it to him reluctantly, still confused. He rotates slowly, the frown never leaving his face. Once the combination is in, he steps back, then motions for me to do the same.

Slowly he steps aside, opening the locker.

There's a *pop!* that startles a few people nearby. Glitter flies out of the locker and into the hallway, just missing Jay.

My eyes widen. "Ohhh . . ."

"Yeah," says Jay. "You're welcome."

Particles of glitter drift toward the lockers beside mine. Those unlucky enough to be standing in front of their lockers at that exact moment get some on their clothes. They brush it off with alarm, sidestepping my locker like the plague.

I tiptoe around the fresh mound of glitter on the floor in front of my locker and peer inside. Everything I have in there is covered in glitter—jacket, books, stickers, cards, basketball shoes. The remains of the explosion mechanism lie there like a culprit—a deflated balloon, a thread connected to my door, and a needle at the end of it. A bomb, in every sense of the word.

I turn to Jay. "Is this—"

"Just our lockers." He nods. "Yep."

"How did you know?"

He shrugs. "You face things like this long enough, you get a sense." He brushes off his jacket. "Lucky you, though. You get to keep your clothes. I just hope there's something decent in lost and found for me." He turns to leave.

"I'm . . . sorry," I say.

He turns back to me. "For what? You didn't do anything."

"Yeah, but . . . for getting you into this. They put it in your locker because you've been helping me."

He frowns. "You know who did this, huh?"

I don't need to have seen them to know. Between them calling me an Oreo and them knowing that Jay brought me onto the team and has been helping me practice, this definitely came from Lee Garroway and the underclassmen on the JV team.

I tell Jay what I'm thinking. He nods.

"That tracks." He motions for me to close the locker and walk with him. "Any idea when they did it?"

"Probably during the home game?"

"Ah. Cos no one's watching the hallways then."

"Exactly. They must've found a way to get into our lockers." I stop him with an arm. "We have to report them, right?"

"Report?" Jay says, then laughs. "Man, you really need some schooling on what it's like out here."

"What d'you mean?"

He pulls me into a corner.

"Listen," he says. "Those guys on the JV team? They're super pissed I'm up there on the subs roster when they can't even cross over. And they're super pissed that you've crawled your way into a seat at the table with them. And now your boy Garroway and them are united in hating us. We didn't make Coach and Mr. Theo choose us, but they don't wanna hear *that*." His voice tightens.

"Also, I hear the Garroway kid's dad is one of the big contributors on the donor roll. Just like Jason's dad and Patrick's dad—all of them, gunning for their sons to make Division I teams, while the rest of us fight for the crumbs. The competition is real, bro, but not for them." He points to us both. "And me and you? Our daddies aren't on the donor list—we earned our spots—so all their frustration comes down on us. No one sees that I don't get off the bench because there's no way up, and no one sees that you being an average player is completely normal. No one cuts us any slack, because no one sees Black boys, except when they want to. And when they see us, it's only to break us. Everyone knows it—Mr. Theo, Coach, Principal Higgins. Do they do anything about it? No. They'd rather just pretend it all away."

He's almost out of breath when he's done, but it leaves me shocked. I've never seen this side of him before, and I'm not sure what to do with it. After a beat or two, I ask the only question I'm thinking.

"So we can't . . . report them?"

"Not without concrete evidence of something really serious," he says. "Or they'll just get a slap on the wrist, and then everyone would know it was us."

"And?"

"*And?* You know what it means to accuse the golden boys of the Hawkins Tigers of something? You're not just accusing them—you'd have to be ready to stand against the team, the school, the town. It's like trying to shoot a pack of wolves—you better be a good shot, and you better not miss."

I run a hand over my head. "Okay, okay. I'll . . . think of another option."

He pats my shoulder. "My man," he says. "Try to spend your time on something else." Then he walks off to lost and found.

The bell for first period goes off before I have a chance to tell him that I may be quitting the team.

...

By the end of the school day, I've figured out a plan to get hard evidence on the Garroway gang. Unfortunately, it involves convincing the most difficult person to convince: Mike.

"Just for a week or something," I say. "Your dad won't even notice."

"That his camcorder is missing?" says Mike. "Oh, Dad will *definitely* notice."

We're in his basement. I told him all about the glitter bombs and everything else that has happened with the Garroway gang so far. I told him about my plan: catch them in the next act—which they'll definitely do once they realize the glitter bomb only worked halfway—all on tape. Turn that tape in to Principal Higgins. Just one problem, though. I need a camcorder to set as a trap in my locker.

"Why not use your mom's?" asks Mike.

"I've told you before—it was a gift from my dad, and my mom forbids us touching anything that's a gift from him," I say. "Also, she would *kill* me if she found out. Your dad may just ground you or something."

"True," says Mike. "But it's just glitter, Lucas. Who cares?"

I leave the Wheeler house crestfallen. He's wrong about

it being *just glitter.* When I get home, I know I have no choice but to do something I've never done—steal Mom's camcorder.

■ ■ ■

Setting it up the next morning is easy. Mom's Handycam is slim enough to look like a paperback novel if placed between other books, and far enough into the locker's shadows. I clear out my locker, scratch my number off the paint, and expand the slits so they're see-through. When I'm done, it looks abandoned.

I make sure all the camcorder's batteries are in, it's turned on, and the lens faces the now wide-open locker door slits. Once I'm sure the camera's running and getting a good shot of the hallway, I shut the locker.

One hundred twenty minutes of recording time, the tapes said. Let's see what I can make of that.

■ ■ ■

Throughout the school day, I change the tapes after every double period. Each time I return to my locker, I ease it open, gently, waiting for something to happen. Nothing. By the end of the day—which also happens to be the end of the fall semester—I've run through five tapes, and there's nothing in them. I inspect every corner of the locker to make sure nothing is booby-trapped there. Turns up clean. I have no choice but to pack up the camera and leave.

On my way to rendezvous with Mike and Dustin, I pass Lee Garroway and his band of friends in the hallway. They don't say hello, and look past me like we didn't just play on the same team days ago. When I go past, they whisper to themselves and laugh.

Lee in particular gives me a lengthy stare, wearing a sly smile on his freckled face. I bet he knows they got to Jay with their glitter. I pat the camera in my backpack. Once the holiday's over and we return to school in the coming year, I'll have found a better way to make sure they don't get off so easy next time.

Turns out I don't have to wait that long.

Three days into the New Year and barely two weeks into the winter holiday, Chief Powell and Officer Callahan show up at our door.

Lucas's guide to surviving freshman year:

- ☑ *Make new friends*
- ☑ *Get out of comfort zone and try new things*
- ☐ *Be yourself*
- ☑ *Avoid relationship and friendship drama*
- ☐ *Remember to live in the moment*

PART THREE

CHAPTER NINETEEN

"A locker exploded at Hawkins High," says Powell. "Home-made bomb."

Chief Calvin Powell has never been one to overreact. From what I understand of the Hawkins Police Department, Hopper was the stubborn, unpredictable one. Phil Callahan, Powell's once partner and now deputy, standing next to him, looks like the aloof member of the bunch. This makes Powell the one with his head squarely on his shoulders. Now I see why he was made chief after Hopper died. But both Powell's and Callahan's signature demeanors have been wiped off as they stand in our front doorway, snow falling lightly onto their jackets, and deliver the news with grim affect.

"May we come in?" Powell says, walking through the doorway before Dad can answer. I'm halfway down the stairs and about to go back up when he spots me and says, "Ah, we'll want to speak to you, too, Lucas, if you don't mind."

I freeze midstep. "Talk to . . . *me*?"

"Yes, son," says Powell, then to Dad, "If we have your permission, Charles."

Dad shoots me a look. My heart skips a beat.

"What did he do?" Dad's voice shifts to the lower register he uses when upset.

"Nothing, nothing," Powell says. "We just need to ask him a few questions about another student."

In no time, we're arranged in the sitting room—me sandwiched between Mom and Dad, Callahan and Powell opposite us with steaming coffee mugs in front of them, and Erica poised in an armchair, watching everything unfold with interest.

"So let me be sure I have this right," Dad is saying. "A high school kid made a bomb at home, rigged it to Lucas's friend's locker, then went away for the holidays?"

"Not quite, but close," says Powell, not touching his coffee.

Callahan, on the other hand, blows steam off the top with intense concentration, as if he'd rather be doing that than talking about a bombing at the high school.

"There must've been some sort of disagreement," says Powell. "That's how these things always start. And so the aggrieved kid goes home, plots revenge, puts some explosives together in his parents' garage, and rigs it to his nemesis's locker at school. But it's the end of the semester, so the school closes. Kid forgets, leaves for winter vacation. And then over the break, when the janitors are prepping for reopening, fumigating and painting lockers, good ol' Reggie finds that one of the lockers has its hinges loosened. Tampered with, as if someone was looking to steal something. So he decides to fix that. He takes the door apart, and just when he pulls it open—" Powell shows his ten fingers. *"Boom!"*

"Oh my God," says Mom. "I hope Reggie's okay?"

"He's a lucky man. The metal door shielded him from most of the explosion. He escaped with a few first- and second-degree burns from the heat but is otherwise fine."

"Holy—" Dad catches himself. "How does a *kid* even make a *bomb?*"

"It's not . . . hard."

This is the first time I've spoken since the police arrived. I've been too shocked, taking this all in, my mind racing through different things without pattern: Jay, Lee Garroway, the MOVE bomb, Uncle Jack's words. I don't know when my mouth opens and words fall out.

Callahan stops blowing on his mug and turns to me. "Is that so?"

"Yeah," I say. "We tried to do it once, my friends and I. Back in sixth grade."

What I don't say is that *I* tried to get my friends to do it after I'd overheard some kids talking about it during Halloween trick-or-treating. I wanted my Rambo costume to be so real that I'd set off a bomb in character. A real bomb. But Will and Mike chickened out and left Dustin and me to do it. We didn't end up doing it, because even though we got the parts we needed from the auto shop, we couldn't get hold of the ether propellant we'd need to make a nice blast, so we abandoned the idea.

"How would you do something like that?" asks Powell, whipping out his notebook. "Wanna run me through it?"

I take him through the materials needed—a metal pipe, gunpowder or propellant, batteries, fuses and a trigger, which I'm guessing in this case was a string tied to the door, just like the glitter bomb. Powell takes this down unceremoniously.

"And just for the record," he says, "you're not the one who planted the bomb in Jermaine Demario's locker, are you?"

I'm taken aback by the question. "Sorry—what?"

"You seem to know a lot about making bombs," Callahan chips in.

"Now, hold on now, Phil," says Dad. "Don't come into my house and accuse my son of things—"

"Charles, relax," says Callahan. "We're not accusing anyone of anything. We're just clarifying."

"Why would I plant a bomb in Jay's locker?" I ask. "He's my *friend*."

"Ah, well, I've seen friends do some nasty things to each other," says Powell. "But I just want it on the record is all."

"Is this an interrogation?" Erica butts in. "Because I know you're not supposed to interrogate a *minor*."

"Should we get a lawyer?" asks Mom.

"People, people," Powell says, rising. "I just need to know Lucas didn't do it so I can have justifiable cause to pursue other leads."

"Jay and I don't mess with people's lockers," I say. "It's *our* lockers that get messed with."

This gets Powell's attention. He sits and whips his book open again. "Wanna repeat that for me, son?"

I freeze, remembering what Jay said about accusing the Garroway gang without evidence.

"You have to tell me, Lucas," Powell nudges. "That's the only way I can bring whoever did this to justice."

"Lucas, if you know something, you better speak now," says Dad.

"I don't know who," I say. "But earlier in the week, someone put a glitter bomb in Jay's locker. And mine."

"Did you report this?" asks Callahan.

I shake my head.

Dad turns to the men. "You spoken to this Jay person, Cal? Or his parents?"

"Oh yes, we've been over at the Demarios'," says Powell,

reaching into his pocket. "In fact, I have something to show you."

He lays a picture on the coffee table, and we all crowd in. The photograph shows the aftermath of the explosion. Soot and scorch marks spread from the locker onto the hallway floor and wall, telling the tale. The blasted door, now warped, is there, blackened. But the photo is focused on what's painted on the inside of the door.

At first, I'm not sure what I'm looking at, because the spray paint has dripped before drying, therefore the graffiti's quite difficult to decipher. Then I realize what it spells at the same time Mom does, with a gasp, and Dad and Erica do, their faces tightened.

My insides recoil.

"Jermaine said he didn't write that," says Powell. "Now, I suspect decent young men don't go around graffitiing slurs on their friends' lockers." He trains his gaze on me. "Especially not *you*. My educated guess is that the same person who rigged that explosion wrote this."

I feel too many things at once—anger, sadness, confusion. Exactly how I felt the first day I heard about the MOVE bombing. I clench my fists to keep my hands from shaking.

"Oh, this is nasty," says Mom, rising, infuriated. "Nasty." She leaves the room.

Dad, whose expression has darkened far more than I've ever seen, says, "Did they write that in my son's locker, too?"

"We didn't check specifically," says Powell, "but I'm guessing not. We scanned every locker and found no incendiaries anywhere else. My guess is, whoever did this was targeting Mr. Demario specifically." He looks at me. "I'm only here because Mr. Demario told us about the glitter bombs and mentioned that your locker was rigged, too. I was hoping you had seen or heard something that may help us." Chief Powell's gaze intensifies. "If there's anything you know that may be of help, now's the time, Lucas."

Everyone's eyes are on me. Even Erica's. I'm thinking hard, wondering if there's a way I can point them in the direction of Garroway and his group, when it suddenly hits me.

I jump to my feet. "The *camera.*"

Powell lifts his eyebrows. "What camera?"

"If I may ask," I say, "when did you say the bomb was put there?"

"Sometime within the last school day, is our guess," says Powell. "Mr. Demario mentioned he didn't open his locker at all on Friday, so we're guessing that saved him and delayed the explosion. I'm sure whoever did this must've known this and maybe tried to get into school later or something, but the building's been locked since that Friday, with only janitorial access to the hallways. Head janitor says no one's allowed in except Principal Higgins. Not even during the basketball games over the break." He pauses. "Why?"

"I think—" My mind races. "I think I may have something."

I go upstairs and return with the camcorder. Mom is back in the living room, and when she spots the camera, she opens her mouth to say something. I'm already rewinding, pushing play, setting it to fast-forward. I put the camcorder on the coffee table and peer at it. Everyone crowds around.

"What're we looking for here . . . ?" Callahan asks, but I just put up a hand. *Wait.*

The video begins, offering us a good view of the hallways, framed by the slits in the locker that I'd beat open. It's clear enough to make out the faces of students as they go by. But more importantly—what they're wearing, and what they're carrying.

"This is all Friday?" Powell asks. I nod. He takes out his notebook, settles in with us, and watches.

The first tape turns up empty—just a bunch of students zipping past the locker at every period bell. The second tape stops right before period ends, and it's unclear how much time is lost before I put in the third tape. The third tape, too, turns up empty, and even shows a recording of me arriving to take it out and put in the fourth.

Then, midway through the fourth tape, I spot something.

It's the middle of the second period after lunch, which means no one should be out. But someone is. A group of *someones.* The group crosses the front of the camera, moving quickly, stealthily.

"Stop!" I lean forward and rewind, pausing when I reach the desired timeline. "There."

Leading the group is Lee Garroway, his freckles unmistakable. And in his hand, also unmistakably identifiable, is a metal pipe.

CHAPTER TWENTY

SATURDAY, JUNE 6, 1981

I don't sleep for the rest of the night. One event from a half decade ago keeps playing in my head, over and over and over.

I've never thought of myself as *the Black kid* at school. I didn't even always think of myself as *a* Black kid. Not until I was nine and Cody Lerner made sure I recognized that part of my identity.

It was the last week of third grade, and the elementary school had put together one last week of activities before most of us went off on vacation. My parents thought this was a good time for me to make new friends ahead of science camp and registered me for a couple of activities, including a Splash into the Summer day of food and games at the community pool. Back then I thought the prospect was absolutely terrifying. I was a weird and awkward kid with no friends (I hadn't met Mike, Will, or Dustin yet). Hanging out at the community pool, surrounded by kids who had grown up together, felt like a death sentence. I'd also been bullied for the first time and was scared of what would happen to me outside of my classroom.

I'd seen Cody around school and whatnot, but he wasn't even one of those jerks I was scared of. He was just a regular glasses-wearing kid whose family had been in Hawkins much longer than mine. Mr. Lerner owned Lerner's, a general store downtown just like Melvald's, only much smaller and with fewer customers. I would soon come to understand why his patronage was not as good.

When the day of the pool event came around, I was nervously curious. I'd never gone to a pool party before. More important, I'd never seen my classmates in anything but school clothes. The promise of seeing them in regular clothes sounded at least intriguing to me. Not until my parents dropped me off with my sitter—the daughter of one of Mom's church friends—and waved goodbye after handing me over did it occur to me that they wouldn't be there.

Luckily, my sitter—I forget her name now, but I remember she was Black—was on top of her game. I remember her asking me my name, telling me to go change. Only at this point did it occur to me that I, too, would have to face my friends in nothing but pool shorts.

I hadn't yet learned to be ashamed of my body, how skinny I am. At the time, many of us were skinny anyway, and the plus-size kids were the ones who got the brunt of bullying about their appearance. Nakedness, or rather the lack of a shirt, did me in. Somehow, being all alone in a sea of people, with shirt and shoes off and the summer heat beating down on my bare back, felt completely isolating.

I made sure to slap on a significant amount of sunscreen, Mom's instructions echoing in my head. Afterward, I got into the water and watched from a distance as a ball game started in the water. Then someone hit the ball too far away, and it floated to me. I picked it up and returned it. To Cody Lerner.

He didn't leave even after hitting the ball back to the players. Instead, he stayed, bobbing up and down in his yellow floating tube—he hadn't learned how to swim yet.

"Aren't you going to wash off?" he blurted out.

I frowned. "Wash off what?"

He pointed at my body. I looked at myself but wasn't sure what he was talking about. Maybe my sunscreen?

"Is it too much?" I asked. "I could always rub it off."

His eyes widened. "You *can*?"

His surprise at my reaction felt weird even then, but I laughed it off.

"Of course I can."

He went back to his game, and I went inside and wiped off some of the sunscreen, cursing myself for overzealously following Mom's directive.

When I returned to the pool, I decided to stay out of the water. I got an ice cream cone from my sitter, found a spot with some shade, and sat with my legs in the water. I'd barely sat half a minute before two girls approached me.

"You have to take your legs out the water," one of the girls, a blond one, said.

I was so unsettled by their instructions that all I could think at the time was: *What in the world is going on?*

I managed to find it in myself to ask: "Why?"

"Cody says you'll wash off," the other girl said. "Into the water."

"Yeah, and we don't want to swim in colored water," the blond girl finished.

"Colored how?" I pressed, then remembered the sunscreen. "I wiped it off."

They eyed me, the blond girl finally saying: "Doesn't seem like you have."

Even though I'd grown more perplexed, I stubbornly refused to take my legs out of the water. They clearly saw this determination and, after a brief moment, swam away and let me be.

But even after they'd left, something in me felt not right. I knew there was something I still wasn't getting about what those kids were saying, but for the life of me, I couldn't process it. So after sitting there for a while and finishing my cone, I decided I'd had enough of that bizarre day and wanted to go home.

Unbeknownst to me, Cody had spread the good news that Lucas Sinclair washes off—*he said so himself!* So when I started to make my way around the pool, back to the changing room, I noticed a difference in everyone's reactions to me.

Every kid—and I mean *every* kid—leaned out of the way when I went by. Some didn't just lean, they outright scampered away when I approached, like I was the bogeyman or something. And then it grew into a spectacle, the Running Away from Lucas Sinclair show. There I was, trying to figure out what the absolute hell was going on— *Did I grow a bad rash in five minutes? Is there something on my face?*—and kids were just having a fun time diving away. All questions, no answers.

My answer came in the form of Cody Lerner himself, who I somehow ran into on my long poolside walk back to my sitter. Unfortunately for him, we met right in the one spot of the walkway where there's not enough room for people to sidestep each other. On one side was a wall, and on the opposite side, the pool, with nothing but a narrow walkway in between. It had exactly enough room for just one person to walk past. If two are going to make it across, it would be a tight fit, and their bodies would likely touch.

Cody froze as I approached. Behind his glasses, his eyes widened with horror.

As much as I was upset by Cody peddling lies, I

remember being prepared to give him room to pass. I'm not sure if the annoyance in my expression put even more pressure on him, but he was absolutely frightened by the very idea of sharing that space with me. Frightened of having any part of his body touch mine. So he looked to the one source of escape left: the pool.

I saw the shift before he jumped, and I thought, *No. He wouldn't.* But jump he did, glasses and all, splashing into the pool.

Except, he jumped into the deep end. And he was without his floating tube. And he didn't know how to swim.

Everything from then on is a blur to me now: the thrashing, calling the lifeguard to attention, multiple bodies jumping in and swimming toward him, fast. I stood there, watching it all in a daze.

After he was pulled out and finished crying snot out of his nose, Cody was asked why he would do such a thoughtless thing. He simply pointed at me.

"He said he could rub off," he said. "I thought he was going to rub off on me."

"What?" The lifeguard was confused, but I wasn't. The real meaning of *rub off* had started to dawn on me.

"Lucas Sinclair," Cody repeated. "I jumped because Dad says to stay away, never to let them touch me. He says if they rub off on me, I better not bring it home."

Thinking back to that moment now, I realize how small the scope of my big-picture understanding was at the time. Even still, I understood enough to know that I didn't want to hear the rest of whatever Cody had to say. I made my way back to the changing room, picked up my stuff, and had my sitter call my parents.

When Mom arrived and asked me what had happened, I told her a boy had almost drowned and it freaked me out, so I wanted to leave. It was not really a lie, but even back then, I somehow knew no amount of conversation with my parents would get me the answers I sought. Maybe I didn't even want answers. Maybe the questions were enough. Maybe that was why, as we rode the rest of the way home that day, I found that I wasn't even upset. Uncomfortable, maybe, but not angry.

If there was something I remember feeling back then, it's the exact same way I feel right now: simply, and completely, exhausted.

CHAPTER TWENTY-ONE

SUNDAY, JANUARY 5, 1986

The weekend following the tape's revelation is a slow, arduous one. Everyone in my house moves like a well-fed fly in the summer. Nobody looks me in the eye. Dad keeps in touch with the police, giving us updates whenever he has them. With Uncle Jack and his antics having returned to Philadelphia, the responsibility to cheer us up falls on Mom. She attacks this problem with her usual solution: baked goods. On a normal day, this would work. But nothing about this situation is normal.

On Sunday afternoon, just one day before school reopens, the weather takes a turn for the worse. Maximum temperatures dip into the low thirties. It doesn't quite snow, but the frost and light dusting is enough to keep us indoors, sapping whatever vibrancy was left from the holiday cheer. A somber disposition takes hold of the house—heck, of Hawkins itself.

Ordinarily, this close to the start of school, I'd be on the phone with Mike and Dustin, planning all the cool ways we'd decorate our lockers for the semester. But I can't even do that—I've been banned from using the phone or calling anyone in the meantime.

Dad, under Chief Powell's advisement, believes it's best if I don't contact Jay until the investigation is over.

I spend most of the day locked in my room, lying in bed and thinking about two people: Jay and Max. I wonder if Jay is doing okay, and what's going to happen when he returns to school. I also wonder if Max is doing okay—if her trailer home has thick enough insulation to withstand the growing cold. But it's less wonder and more just wishing she was here with me. I hum Kate Bush silently, thinking about the last time she let me hold her hand.

It was last summer, at Starcourt, before everything else happened. We were getting ice cream. Her palm was so soft, I said I wanted to order it as a flavor. She laughed. It sounded like the birds from *Cinderella*.

Erica drops in at some point, something she never does unless it's to bug me for some reason. This time, though, she only perches on the edge of the bed, watches me for a moment, and speaks all of four words.

"A bomb, huh?" she says. "Sick."

I'm not sure if she means *sick* as in *awesome,* or *sick* as in *horrible,* but I guess it can be both with Erica. I don't ask, and she doesn't explain. We sit in silence, watching the ceiling together until she gets bored and leaves.

The wind picks up as the day goes on. Weather forecast says there's going to be storms for the rest of the week, and we're advised to crank up the heat and keep an eye out for frozen pipes. Between all this, Dad gets some news from the police: Lee Garroway has been taken into custody.

"Cal says the evidence is solid enough, and the boy has confessed," Dad tells Mom, though we listen in. "Looks like four counts. Arson, burglary, attempted assault, possession of explosive devices."

Now that I'm free from the phone ban, I call Jay's house a bunch of times. No one picks up. Perhaps something to do with the storm. I decide to just wait and see Jay in school.

An hour before bedtime, while I'm poring over my closet for what to wear the next day, Dad comes to my room and stands at the doorway.

"Did I ever tell you," he says, "that I used to be a barber?"

I look up. "No?"

"I was a good one, too." He steps into the room, moving slowly as if not to alert me. "Gave cuts for a dollar or two long before the Supercuts came along." He stops before me and touches my now-overgrown hair lightly, massages it carefully with his fingers. "What do you say I give you a fresh cut tonight?"

My eyes widen. Dad has never cut my hair or declared any interest in doing so. When I was younger, Mom would take me with her to the salon, and they'd snip it with scissors, until I grew old enough to go to the barbershop myself. Between starting high school, basketball practice, and the cold winter, I haven't visited in a while. And now my hair has grown into a wild, untamed Afro. Dad's right. I could do with a trim.

"Okay," I say.

His eyes light up at the thought. "I'll go get my kit."

The "kit" is a loose assortment of tools. A series of combs, brushes and picks, a straight razor, a clipper. He also arrives with two mirrors—a large one for him, and a small one for me. I never even knew we had such things in this house. But it turns out Dad's been cutting his own hair all along. And here I was, thinking that he had his own private barber or something.

"Okay, so what we thinking?" he says. "Got any ideas?"

I shake my head. "Not really."

"How about a high-top fade?"

I turn my head around and look at him. "Are you . . . sure?"

"Yeah," he says. "It's what these hip-hop kids and NBA stars are wearing nowadays, right? Has to be cool or something." He manages a smile, but I don't quite return it.

"You don't like hip-hop stars." I say this more matter-of-factly than I intend. "Or basketball stars."

"Well, I don't like a lot of things," he says, turning me

around to face the mirror. "But that shouldn't prevent you from enjoying them."

He places a towel on my neck and prepares his tools.

The haircut is soothing and calm, a far cry from the wind baying outside. Dad hums some old-timey tune as he cuts, stopping every now and then to check for alignment. When he stops humming, the gentle whir of the clipper settles between us.

"I don't hate being Black," he says, out of nowhere.

Mom, I think. Of course she told him about our talk.

"I want you to know that," he continues as he cuts. "And maybe I haven't done a good job of showing you that in the past. But I want you to know, now, that I love and am proud of who I am. I love being African American. And no matter what anyone says to you—I want you to love it too."

I nod, but he holds my head to straighten it while he cuts.

"Why are you always angry, then?" I ask. "At Uncle Jack. At Black people? At . . ." I pause. "Your . . . foster parents."

He says nothing for a while. I can hear his breathing, even and shallow over my head, contained. When he eventually speaks, it's with his soft voice.

"There's something you learn very early about being us, Lucas," he says, calling me by my name for the first time in a long time. "As a Black person in this world, you're always out there trying to live, but you're forced to spend so much time surviving." He pauses. "All I've ever wanted for you—for everyone in this house—is to live without always having to be told that all we must do is survive."

He brushes over my neck, takes off the towel, then hands me the small mirror. I check out the haircut from multiple angles. It's very Grace Jones, but taller because my hair is a lot fuller. It's very NBA, very hip-hop, very *cool*.

"You like it?" Dad asks.

"Yeah," I say, looking up to him. "Yeah, I love it. Thanks, Dad."

"You're welcome, son." He packs up his tools to go, stops at the door, turns. He looks like he's about to say something big and weighty and difficult, to expel a burden off himself. But it never comes. Instead, he says: "Try cleaning up all that hair on the floor before going to bed, will you?"

CHAPTER
TWENTY-TWO

A LONG, LONG TIME AGO

After I get into bed, I think about all of Dad's silences—
tonight, but also over the years. I think of all the things
left unsaid, and all the things he would like to share but
can never bring himself to say. I think of the story of how
we got to Hawkins, the only story about ourselves that my
parents *never* tell.

What led to Erica and me asking about this part of our
history was noticing that we didn't have extended family around. This was long before Uncle Jack. Like Erica,
I saw that most people around had generations of their
family close by. Often right here in Hawkins, even though
they sometimes lived in separate houses. Sometimes nearby

family lived just outside town; sometimes, as far away as Indianapolis. Many had siblings and cousins in towns along the state lines in places like Michigan, Ohio, Kentucky, Illinois. This was because most people who stayed in Hawkins simply remained, and those who didn't simply left. It's very rare for someone in Hawkins to keep in touch with family that doesn't live nearby.

Not us, though. For a long, long time, it was just Mom, Dad, Erica, and me. Then the Veterans Administration chapter in Indiana offered a program for all who'd previously served abroad and returned to retrace any family they might have lost in the meantime. Dad took advantage of it, and the state helped him locate Uncle Jack.

Dad talks about his days as a kid sometimes, but not very often. Between him and Uncle Jack, I get the feeling that their birth father did not like to talk much about himself either. The only thing Dad would sometimes talk about was something called the Great Migration, which I understand to be how his family left the South and moved northward. What city in the South their family moved from, Dad and Uncle Jack could never say, as they were much too young when it happened. Their family got separated during the move and ended up scattered all over the place. That was how Dad lost Uncle Jack in the first place. Whether they had been actually abandoned or just lost, Dad never said. I'm not sure if he doesn't know, or doesn't want to be confronted with a painful truth.

Either way, Mom, more sympathetic to our curiosities, told us the rest of the story. Dad ended up in foster care, and because his birth papers had also been lost during the family's move, he was bounced from foster home to foster home in various cities until the state could find a permanent place for him. Some of this meant living with entirely new families at various times, and most of them treated him badly. I remember asking: *Like a slave?* We'd just begun to learn about slavery in school, and the concept was still fresh in my mind.

Mom's response was calm, but too measured and calculated to be revealing the whole truth.

"Not really," she'd said. "Not really."

Finally, Dad ended up in New Jersey when he was seven, after which he was adopted by a white family. In this house, we call them Dad's Foster Parents, and nothing else. He has never referred to them as his father or mother or our grandparents. He never let us even think of them as Grandma or Grandpa. He gets incensed when we speak about them at all, and warns us never, *ever* to bring those memories into our house.

Mom said he left them once he was eighteen and joined the army because that was the only place he could make good money with his not-so-great grades from public high school. He was shipped off to Arlington, Virginia, then Vietnam. *I was lucky to come back,* Dad says often. And though I've always had access to most of his war paraphernalia, it only recently began to strike me as note-worthy that he never tells stories of his time there except for when he's trying to teach us a lesson.

Mom, on the other hand, was happy to tell us about Arlington, Virginia, where *she* happened to grow up. First thing she and Dad had bonded over when they met, she said. She reminisced about her childhood: going to church and having Sunday cookouts afterward, getting stuffed on potato salad and BBQ and mac and cheese and corn bread and peach cobbler, her mother going home with Tupper-ware full of even more. She talked about double-Dutching in the streets in hot summers, the fire hydrants turned on, kids putter-pattering barefoot in the water, laughter gliding along with the heat waves. She talked about waiting at the salon for her mother to get her hair done, the smell of re-laxer and hair grease piercing her nostrils as she idly leafed through the heaps of glossy magazines scattered around, idolizing the models with smooth skin and wondering what it would take to get hers to shine like that.

But just like with Dad's refusal to speak about his past, I couldn't help but feel that something about that picture was missing on purpose. Just like Hawkins has begun to feel to me in recent days, it feels like there's something underneath that memory. This utopia Mom paints sounds so far away, a distant land of mystery, even though it's only a couple of states away.

It's just like the Upside Down of Hawkins, isn't it? Dan-ger's never truly distant. There's a monster under our collective beds that no one wants to acknowledge exists. And every now and then, when something tilts our world just a bit too far, the face of the monster comes slipping out, baring its teeth.

Sometimes my parents tell themselves stories when they think we're asleep. They whisper, as if speaking too loud will bring this monster out from under the bed. Voices lowered behind shut doors, whispering words like *Klansman* and *Confederate* and *segregated*. Their voices quaver, and they sigh after, and there's relief under their words, like they finally escaped something.

Mom says most of her family remained in Arlington, but she and her parents moved to Philadelphia for better opportunities. It was there she had gone to typing school and ended up with enough skills to perform different secretarial duties. Oddly enough, it was also there she'd met Dad, who, once he'd returned from the war, tried to find new work in Philadelphia because New York City was too crowded. They clicked, and got married.

That's where the story ends, though. They don't talk about why we didn't stay in Philadelphia, or go back to Arlington, or what prompted them to move to middle-of-nowhere Hawkins especially while Mom was pregnant. They don't talk about how the neighbors welcomed or didn't welcome them, or how hard or easy it was to settle in. They don't talk about why Mom sometimes calls her hairdresser Sista Rosie rather than just Rosie. They don't talk about if they ever feel alone in Hawkins, if they ever feel like they're different, if they're ever made to feel like freaks just for *being*.

Now that I understand all of Dad's silences, the word *Black* holds weight in a way it never has for me before. Now I understand why we don't talk about being Black in our house, or existing as Black people, being Black people. Maybe they've always been afraid that if we mention the word, the monster would come out from underneath the bed, just like it has for Jay with this homemade bomb. Maybe that's the biggest reason, more than any, that Dad freaks out whenever Uncle Jack comes visiting. Maybe Uncle Jack is a just a reminder to him that we can't hide and pretend forever.

I've never thought of my parents as afraid. But I remember exactly how I felt the first time I saw the Demogorgon. I completely lost the ability to make a sound. I guess when there's a monster under your bed all the time, you lose the ability to speak.

CHAPTER TWENTY-THREE

MONDAY, JANUARY 6, 1986

The storm does not let up by the next morning, and neither does my anxiety. Mom calls ahead, hoping the school will designate a snow day, but apparently it's hard to call a snow day without snow. So we end up driving to school through the bad weather, crawling up the road like tortoises. I relish the delay. Every second that takes me closer to school is agony. I feel like throwing up.

A year or two ago, I would never have thought a back-to-school morning would make me feel this way.

As soon as I get out and brave the cold from car to entrance hallway, I spot Mike and Dustin. Relief washes over me like a wave, and the tightness in my chest releases.

I've never been more excited to see my friends. I feel like crying.

We say hello, riffing through pleasantries. Little seems to have changed with them.

"Crazy winter break, am I right?" I say.

Mike squints. "What do you mean? Break was fine."

"Yeah," says Dustin. "Spent it talking to Suzie. When she wasn't at worship service."

"Same," says Mike. I realize he looks a lot more chipper than before. Much too chipper for this weather. "El and I sent a bunch of letters. *Love* letters, you know? It was awesome." He looks at me. "What about yours?"

We're walking into the school now, and as we get to the hallway, it starts to dawn on me what has happened.

The hallway is bright and colorful. All the lockers wear a fresh coat of paint, as do some of the walls. No locker numbers are missing. The floor is shiny and polished, no skid marks. Cherry-cheeked students, blushing from both the cold outside and the excitement of seeing their friends for the first time in the New Year, glide across the floors.

They don't know. *No one* knows.

It makes sense now. Jay had been right about that golden boy stuff. Garroway's parents would never want this to come to light, if they could help it. Maybe they even paid to clean up the mess real quick. That's the only way this hallway is a far cry from what I saw in the photo Chief Powell showed us. A free touch-up and unpaid repairs may have been too big of an offer for Principal Higgins to refuse. And now, it's like nothing even happened, like everything that I went through—that Jay went through—never happened.

It's like the Upside Down all over again. Except I've been the only one lost in it the whole time, and now I've only just woken up to the real world.

My friends are still going on about their holidays, but I've stopped walking.

"Lucas?" says Dustin. "Lucas?"

"You okay, man?" Mike is asking.

I realize I've reached my locker, am standing in front of it, unable to touch or open it.

"Listen," Dustin is saying, "Eddie's set up our first Hellfire game of the semester today. Lucky you, we're in need of a sub. You can jump in literally today!"

I look around me, checking to see if I'll spot Jay around or something. His locker, in the far end of the hallway, looks intact. He's nowhere to be found, though.

"Lucas, are you *listening*?" says Dustin.

"Yes, yes," I say. "I'll come for your stupid Hellfire game." Then I trudge off to Mr. Lansdale's class without putting away my books or jacket.

■ ■ ■

Hellfire Club is exactly what the name suggests: a collection of freaks and nerds in the AV room.

Back in middle school, whenever other kids would call

us freaks, I always thought we were the definition of what *freak* looked like. Kids who loved movies, fantasy games, the arcade, and science fairs. But in observing the group before me now, I realize that these guys are what most people would consider true freaks.

There's the Eddie Munson dude, to start. Long-haired, sporting the usual metal band T-shirt, wearing a guitar pick around his neck and looking like he hasn't taken a shower all winter break. His pals Gareth and Jeff are spitting images, just with shorter hair. The rest of Hellfire is a smattering of sophomores to seniors, but they're all the same—people who don't *fit*. In fact, for the first time, I see me and my friends as . . . normal. Sure, we may be weird, but no way in hell we're *weirdos* like these.

But they've invited me anyway, so I show. Surprisingly, Eddie Munson, who's Dungeon Master, has little to say to me. He just bids me welcome and asks me to join Mike and Dustin's group. Leader of the group is Gareth, supported by Jeff. They all welcome me, then hand me the character sheet to fill out before joining in the quest.

The campaign is called Vecna's Curse and follows the dark, one-eyed, one-armed wizard Vecna and his band of cultists. There's a painting of the dude done by some really talented artist. For a moment, I just stand there and gaze at the rendition of this spellcasting dark wizard, tentacles sticking out of him like an octopus, his roving eye and wizened hand too real-like for my taste. It reminds me too much of the Upside Down and all the minions its ruler has sent so far to decimate this town and my friends. I wonder if the Mind Flayer has someone like Vecna in his arsenal, just waiting for the right time to unleash him.

I tear my gaze away and focus on completing my character information. I opt for my most stock character, who I'd pick even to battle the Mind Flayer himself. A fast, keen, and sneaky fighter who can be relied upon by allies and will always use their power to do what's right, but who's just as quick and deadly to turn against those who come for them. For this campaign, I choose a Level Two Elven Fighter with a Criminal background. For ability scores, I go with a standard array of 15 Strength down to 8 Charisma because I don't have time. I quickly choose equipment: crowbar, hood and pouch of gold from my criminal past, and a greatsword and shield for the campaign. For personality traits, I have two go-tos: *always have a plan for when things go wrong* and *making a new friend is better than making a new enemy*. For ideals, I have only one: *stealing from the wealthy to help those in need*. Finally, I settle on a name for my character: *Gramnur*.

For a straight period, we battle. The d20 rolls on the board, clacking and clacking, as we wade through forests, charge down hills, climb up city walls, slice through armies. For the whole hour, the troubles of the world outside the AV room disappear, and I'm fully immersed, realizing how much I've missed this game.

But then the bell for the end of lunch period goes off, and we're forced to suspend until our next meeting. We high-five each other, all of us, and talk excitedly about what spells we should've used, what damage we'll cause next time. Eddie and Gareth invite me for the next meeting. Mike and Dustin are thrilled.

But as I walk out of the door of that AV room, into the hallway, and back to my locker, the color drains from everything as I remember. I stop short, turn around, and look at the sophomore lockers. Still no Jay. I decide I'll use Mike or Dustin's locker in the interim, but I suddenly remember that Max's locker is nearer to mine.

But Max is also nowhere to be found.

■ ■ ■

Max and I haven't spoken since our breakup. Before the winter break, I said hello to her a few times in the hallways, but she only ever responded with a weak smile. I didn't push, though. She asked for space, and I've got to respect that. But I would be lying if I said a huge part of me didn't want to go right back and try again and again until she'd talk to me.

The truth is: I miss her.

I spent most of the winter break thinking about what she was doing for Christmas, if she was even having a good holiday season at all. My hands itched to pick up the phone and call her, just to know that she was okay. But I promised myself that I'd give her the time to work through all the stuff happening in her life, and when she was ready she'd come to me. Not like that would stop me from thinking about her, though.

For the rest of the day, my mind alternates between Jay and Max, the euphoria of the D&D game all but forgotten. When I went and asked at the front desk, it turned out Jay is not just absent from his locker—he's absent from school altogether. *On the first day after break?* Something is up at the Demario house, and no one's talking.

After the bell for the end of school rings, Mike and Dustin ride off with Nancy. I'm stuck waiting for Mom in the parking lot. That's when I spot Lee Garroway. He's being escorted from the school premises by a teacher, into an expensive-looking car I think might be his dad's. I realize now that I didn't see him in any classes. Is that his punishment—taking classes privately? *That's it?* My neck grows hot at the thought. He's walking away scot-free, really.

Around me, other students gossip.

"Heard he's on house arrest," says one.

"I hear he wears an electronic monitor on his ankle," says another.

"Wonder what he did to get kicked off the team," says a third.

When Mom picks me up, I ask her what the police have said about Jay.

"Nothing," she says. "Though I hear they kicked out all the boys who were involved, except the Garroway boy. His father made some kind of deal, I don't know. Your dad tried to ask Cal, but he says it's above him and he can't say. About your friend, though—I'm not sure."

All the way home, I clench my teeth. I can't believe I get to go back to school and face this Lee kid every day. And worse, I can't really talk to anyone about it—if no one at school knows, then all of this is being kept secret for some reason. Can't tell my friends because I dunno when Dustin's big mouth's gonna let something slip, and I can't tell Max because she's nowhere to be found. There's only one person who I can talk about this to, who already knows, and who'll understand what I'm feeling.

Whatever the situation at the Demario house is, I no longer care. I'm going out there to see Jay.

CHAPTER
TWENTY-FOUR

SATURDAY, JANUARY 11, 1986

The Demario house is on Monroe, which makes me glad I didn't tell anyone I was coming here. If Dad found out I was on this side of the tracks, he'd be furious. All the streets crossing Broadway this far north—Johnson, Washington, Madison—hold at least one building that's a warming center or for emergency housing. All the Hawkins "undesirables," the ones who wouldn't be let within breathing distance of neighborhoods like Loch Nora—and if I was being honest, streets like mine, to a greater or lesser extent—often end up packed here. Most of the housing is also sprawling state-funded projects. They aren't in any way bad, from the look of them. Just simply cheaper. Must be why most of us have come to associate this part of town with, well, poverty.

It surprises me that Jay lives in one of these apartments. He's never given me the impression that his family lacked money, and from the way he dressed—always neat, always put together—I'd never know. I realize now that maybe the problem is not Jay, but me—us—and how I've interpreted his family's status just because of where he lives. I smack myself mentally for jumping the gun. Maybe this is a good lesson for me to remember: that if I expect others to refrain from passing value judgment on me, I have to first learn to stop passing it on others so quickly.

I knock at the door with a plastic knocker painted in copper. A moment passes, then a shadow darkens the light beneath the door. It opens halfway, then completely to reveal a tall, light-skinned Black man, who I guess is Mr. Demario, Jermaine's father.

He looks surprised to see me, but like how someone would be surprised if a long-lost friend turned up at their door. There's a hint of recognition in his eyes. I'm not sure if it comes from him realizing I must be the Lucas his son spoke to the police about, or because there probably haven't been a lot of young Black Hawkins boys standing at this door.

"Good day, sir," I say, remembering my home training. "My name is Lucas Sinclair, and I'm here to see Jermaine. I'm his teammate from school."

He tilts his head just that little bit slightly. "Teammate, eh? You one of the ones who put a bomb in his locker?"

My eyes widen at the suggestion. "I would never, sir."

He assesses me and seems to accept that I'm okay after all. But he isn't done with the questions.

"Are you a friend of his?" he asks.

I frown. "Yes?"

"Are you *a friend*?" he repeats, gazing more intently at me.

The reality of what he's asking dawns on me then. And he's right to ask. I'm still a jock, am I not? There's nothing to prove I'm better than—or different from—those jocks back at school.

Mr. Demario holds the door and waits for me to respond.

"I would never do anything to hurt Jay" is all I finally manage.

Mr. Demario looks me over again, then sighs, shaking his head.

"At least he got to meet one sensible brother here." Then he leans back and shouts toward the stairs: "Jermaine! You got a friend at my door." He returns to me and flashes a small smile. "He'll be down with you in a minute."

He leaves me standing there on the porch, door open in invitation. Mom's voice comes on in my head, reminding me never to go into another person's house without an invitation. So I wait for Jermaine to come out.

A window opens overhead. I look up into the face of a girl who's maybe eight or nine. She wears cornrows in the front half of her head, and has Afro puffs on either side for the back, held by colorful ties. She doesn't say anything, just stares at me, expressionless.

"Hi?" I say, and wave awkwardly. She doesn't respond. I stare at the open door and into the hallway, with its stack of umbrellas and hung coats. But the silence doesn't last long. Soon a question floats down to me from above.

"Do you play basketball like Jay-Jay?"

I look up. My mouth opens, seeking an answer but finding none.

"Anita." Jay's voice echoes as I hear footfalls on the stairs. He appears at the bottom, dressed in jogging pants and a casual T-shirt, like he hasn't left his bed all day. His hair is pressed on one side, telling me he probably hasn't. He smiles at me in welcome but takes some time to poke his head out the front door and look upward.

"What did I say about harassing my friends from the window?" he asks.

"I was only asking a question," the girl says.

"How would you like it if I asked *your* friends questions when they came?"

"They would answer? Isn't that why they have mouths?"

There's so much familiar about this interaction that, for a moment, it feels interchangeable with my house. Then the little girl—Anita—kisses her teeth and shuts the window with a snap, and I'm jerked back, standing in front of Jay again.

"Hey, man," he says, then pauses. "Wild break, huh?"

I breathe. "Yeah."

"Nice fade, too. Where'd you get that done?"

"My dad."

"For real? Wanna trade him for my pops?" Jay chuckles, but I only manage a smile. He notices my countenance.

"Come on," he says, but doesn't bring me into the house. He shuts the door and points me to a nearby tree with a tire swing hanging from it.

■ ■ ■

"What do you mean *not coming back*?"

I'm sitting at the foot of the tree, but Jay stands in the tire, swinging to and fro like a person without worries. I'm surprised by how calmly he's taking all of this. I'd be completely freaking out if I were him.

Jay pushes himself forward. "Just what it means. My folks say it's too dangerous to go back if Lee Garroway's still there. Who knows what he'll do next?"

"Well, *I'm* still there, and nothing's happened so far."

He pushes himself forward. "But aren't you . . . scared?"

I take too long to answer and he cocks his head. "Bingo."

He stops swinging and waits for the tire to come to a halt, then sits in it instead, swaying slightly from side to side.

"It's not the first time for us, you know?" he says. "I never told you what made us move out of Cleveland, but . . ." He looks up to the sky. "And it wasn't just me, back there. My mother, my father, even Anita. Everywhere we went—at school, at work, at home, at the grocery store—there was always someone ready to remind us of what we looked like. To try to convince us that no matter who we were and what we did, they would always be better than us. And whenever we rejected this lie, we got punished." He shakes his head. "The only way to survive was to leave."

I'm not sure what to say, so I stay silent.

"My dad thought that we could do with a fresh start in some middle-of-nowhere place. We thought that at least if people in a town like Hawkins thought being Black was a crime, they'd be too polite to come up in our faces and say it. And honestly, he was right . . . to a degree. No one has straight up walked up to me and talked shit to my face." He chuckles. "Now that I think of it, maybe I'd have preferred that to someone trying to obliterate me like the folks at Osage Avenue."

I've never thought of Hawkins as a place of solace, where one goes to find something they cannot find in the outside world. But as Jay speaks, a lightbulb turns on somewhere in my mind. Maybe I've been unable to see this town as the upside down it's always been because I've lived in it all along. It's like gravity. Everyone in the world thinks they're right-side up, even though they're not. No one wants to face the truth that the monster under their bed is there because it finds comfort in their house.

"I don't know how you picked towns," I say, "but you picked a shit one."

Jay bursts out laughing. It catches me by surprise, and I end up joining in the laughter. Afterward, he sighs, smiles.

"Yeah," he says. "Sometimes, it's the hope that gets you."

We sit in silence and I'm back at ease. Talking to Jay feels like staring into a parallel dimension, one where I can see all of myself. Now I finally understand my frustrations with Mike and Dustin—and to a lesser extent, Max—and how they can never understand what it means to be me and make the choices I do, no matter how much I try to explain it. In the same way that Jay's experience in Hawkins is different from mine even though we're both Black boys who go to the same high school, my friends have understandings of our town that are completely foreign to me, even though we all grew up here.

"Do you think it's possible to care about something that also sucks?" I ask.

"Totally," says Jay. "That's how I feel about basketball."

I lift my eyebrows. "Really?"

"For real. I love it, but sometimes, it's just . . . too much. All the fashion, the intensity, the drama, the expectations. Basketball is literally what got me into this school in the first place, and now it's going to be the same reason I can't go back."

"Yeah," I say. "I feel the same way about Hawkins. This

town is everything I know, and everyone I love and care about lives here." I sigh. "But these days, I feel like if something's gonna be the end of me, it'll be this town, too, you know?"

"It probably is," says Jay. "Just silently."

"And with a smile," I add.

Another period of silence passes before I ask the question I've been holding in.

"So you're leaving."

"Yeah." It's not really a question, and Jay doesn't treat it as one. The little hope I have left splatters to the ground.

"School, or the town?" I ask.

He shrugs. "Not sure there's much I can do in town if I don't go to the only school here."

"Where will you go?"

"Dunno. We haven't figured it all out yet, but . . . we'll see." He looks at me. "What I'm more interested in is— what will *you* do?"

"I don't understand."

He adjusts himself in the tire. "You ever wonder why I've been helping you?"

I *have* wondered. In the beginning, I was simply glad to hang out with him. But as the days went on, I began to think about why he chose to continue, even after the official peer mentor period was over. But I shake my head so he can explain it.

"I know you say this town ain't shit," he says, "but one thing I know is that it remembers its own. I moved here from the outside, so no matter how hard I try, I'm always a visitor. But *you*—see, you're part of the fabric of this place. Hawkins may not like you or enjoy your presence, but Hawkins gotta deal with you, since you're not going anywhere. You're Hawkins through and through. So I thought: If I'm not allowed to fully be the person I want to be here, if I can't get on the starting team because I'm some Black kid from Cleveland—maybe Lucas Sinclair will."

Truth dawns on me now. I'd always thought the animosity from the sophomores on the JV team was just about him getting past them and onto the varsity roster. But no. It was about him being Black and an outsider and *still* outshining them.

Now it makes sense why they bombed and graffitied his locker and not mine. In their eyes—and in the eyes of Hawkins—my Black is different from Jay's Black. That *same-but-different-ness* is what we, the Sinclairs, have always represented in this town. This is what Dad, I think, has been trying to tell me all along—to remember that even though Hawkins isn't as safe for me as I'd like, it's probably the lesser of two evils.

"I was worried for a while there, though," Jay's still saying. "That I was pushing you toward something you didn't want to do, or that wasn't good for you. You know how once you get a little tall as a Black boy, everyone thinks you *have* to be a basketballer by all means."

"Nah." I shake my head. "I didn't feel pressured or anything. Not by you."

"I wanted to step back sometimes, you know?" he says. "But I eventually decided that not creating that space for you to try out everything you wanted to, not sending the ladder down, in a way—that'd be a true disservice, you know?"

I nod. He's not wrong. I *do* want to get out of my comfort zone and try everything, *be* everything. Just like he gets to. I definitely wouldn't have wanted to be kept away. My parents have been trying to keep me away from the world outside Hawkins most of my life. Look how that's worked out for all of us.

"The Tigers are gonna struggle without you," I say. "You know we're only doing so well this season because, for the first time, the starting team has high-quality subs, right? Of which you are one?"

He chuckles. "Yeah, I guess. Coach is def furious. Called my folks already, like, twice. Apparently, half the bench and JV team are both shaved now that they've chunked Garroway's allies out of school. They'll have to recruit straight from JV. Who knows—maybe you'll even get a shot!"

"Ha," I say. "Impossible."

"If you've learned anything so far, it's that nothing is," he says. "If you get the call, take it. My one rule is to never lock yourself out of anything. You never know—maybe basketball will end up doing for you what you've always wanted it to." He smiles. "Too bad I won't be there to see it."

We sit in silence for a while longer. I wonder if my reason for coming here is too selfish if I can't even offer him some solace. But I think both of us kinda needed this. We may be two different Black boys in middle-of-nowhere Hawkins, but we're two different Black boys who have chosen the path of defying the world.

Jay looks up, back into the trees. "Promise me one thing, though?"

"What?"

"Keep your head on your shoulders?" he says. "Garroway and them's just the first. There's gonna be more out there. Monsters peeking out of every corner. Easy to see those coming from afar. But sometimes they get close, you know? So you've gotta watch yourself. Before you open your mouth and call anyone *friend,* make sure they do the work to earn that title. That's the only way to be sure you'll never get burned."

I want to ask him for more advice. *How do I go back to opening my locker without panicking? How do I return to the team if I'm asked? How do I get better at basketball?* But it feels selfish. Throughout the time Jay's been helping me, he's had to deal with all this major stuff as well. Despite that, it never showed in his behavior. He was never mean to me because the world was against him. Maybe it's time I start to learn to paddle my own boat in the same way.

"Nah," I say, drawing out the *ah* in an imitation of him. He laughs in response.

"I think you have enough going on right now. Anything I have, I'll deal with on my own." I pause. "You think we'll see each other again?"

He shrugs. "My folks are kinda known for moving fast with their decisions, so . . ."

"This is . . . goodbye?"

"Honestly?" he says. "I dunno. But it may be wise to treat it like so."

We shake hands. It's not intimate, but it's not sad either. It's two dudes knowing the world will always ask them to prove themselves, so they're saying to each other, *Here's some strength and spirit to help you take that on.*

CHAPTER TWENTY-FIVE

TUESDAY, JANUARY 14, 1986

I'm in the middle of English class when my name is announced on the PA system. For a moment, I'm in shock, wondering what I've done now to be called in by Principal Higgins, when I realize I'm not being summoned to the principal's office. I'm being called into the sports office.

Coach—whose name I've never known and never bothered to ask because I don't think anyone knows anyway—is seated behind his small desk in a stall-like room when I arrive. He wears a polo shirt and sports some weekend stubble, making him look like some random dad in my neighborhood, a far cry from the man I often see courtside, pacing in tracksuits and yelling at everyone possible.

"You asked to see me?" I say to get his attention.

"Sinclair," he says, looking up, then waving me to a seat. I drop into the nearest one.

"I just want to say," he starts, "what an unfortunate turn of events we've experienced, those boys breaking into lockers and . . . everything." I notice he doesn't outright mention the bomb, which makes sense. Everyone at Hawkins High thinks Garroway and the sophomores got axed for "breaking and entering." Everyone except Coach and Principal Higgins, probably.

"Now, you might've noticed how well we're doing this season—unprecedented, really," he continues. "Then suddenly, we're short of players. Which means we need to draw a few backups from JV and throw y'all into subs. Just in case." He pulls out a lined record book and flips through it. "Now, Mr. Theo tells me you're one of the few on the squad with a level head. Told him I don't need no youngsters with too much blood rushing into their brains who'll come in and mess up my team. He says to take a look at you." He looks up to me. "Well, I'm looking. Is there anything I'm not seeing, Sinclair?"

"Sir?" I'm still processing the barrage of information. *Me? Pulled up to varsity?*

"Are you going to mess up my team, son?"

"No, no," I say. "I, uh, know some of the starters well. Jason and Patrick and Andy."

"And have you followed our games all season?"

"Yes. I listen to the radio when I can't be there in person. The reporters say we're showing championship-winning form."

"Eh, don't believe everything you hear," he says, then smirks. "But, yes, we are." He snaps the book shut. "Well, seems to me like you're a responsible young man with his head on his shoulders. I know you're no Michael Jordan, but that bench needs filling, so I will see you at first team practice next week."

I walk back to class, dazed. During lunch period, I catch up with Mike and Dustin and tell them the news. They're not thrilled. In fact, they immediately remind me of my obligations to Hellfire.

"You just got *in,*" says Mike. "Now you wanna run back out to the team that literally hates you?"

"It's not the *same* team," I insist. "That was JV. This is a whole other team."

"But what's the difference?" asks Dustin. "Aren't they all jocks?"

"More like all jackasses," Mike adds.

"Hey," I say. "You've met Jay. Would you call him a jackass?"

"One good apple in a rotten barrel doesn't make it a good barrel of apples, Lucas," says Dustin.

"You're still going to show up for Hellfire, right?" Mike asks. "If you don't, we'll have to explain to Eddie why you bailed. *Again.*"

"Well, how about this?" I point to them with my plastic fork. "You *both* show up to my games, then I show up to Hellfire. Call it even."

After lunch, I see Max for the first time in weeks. She doesn't look any better than the last time I saw her—in fact, she may look even more out of sorts. I want to dash across the hallway, hold her hand, and ask her if she's okay, if there's anything I can *be* for her right now. But she disappears behind a classroom door before the thought is complete.

I make a mental note to leave a message in her locker. But the day gets ahead of me and I completely forget. Only while biking home do I remember, and as I smack myself for forgetting, it strikes me:

I didn't just forget to slip Max the note. I forgot *about* Max.

CHAPTER TWENTY-SIX

THURSDAY, OCTOBER 31, 1985

Last Halloween, before we broke up, Max told me she was going to run away.

It wasn't the first time. She said the last time she had tried to run away, the police had found her at the train station and brought her back home. Her mother was furious, stepdad even more so, and Billy the most furious because he got blamed for not keeping a good enough eye on her. This time, he was gone, and there would be no one for her parents to blame besides themselves. More important, her intention this time was to never be found.

I didn't ask her what she was running away from. Who wouldn't want to run away and leave Hawkins behind? The

Byerses did it already, and more were doing it every day. If I lived in a house with an empty room because the person who used to live there was killed by a Spider Monster from another dimension, I would want to run away, too.

But I knew it wasn't just about Billy. Since the phone call I'd made to her house back then, I started to understand that there was something off about Neil. I've never met him, but I've heard enough stories—gossip at Melvald's about Susan Hargrove. I've seen the way Max flinches when anyone mentions Neil or calls her *Maxine* like he does—same way she flinches when people stop her to say, *I'm sorry about your brother.* I know she's still mad at her mother for making them move to Hawkins in the first place. I know she's mad at the world because she keeps losing people.

So even before Robin gave me that good advice, I did nothing else but listen that day. All Max wanted was for me to follow her to the bus station, and I did just that. In the silence between us, she did all the explaining. She talked about how she'd planned this for Halloween night because everyone would be out, and no one would be looking for her until it was too late. She'd planned to dress as Green Lantern for Halloween because Wonder Woman costumes weren't her thing. I chuckle now, remembering that. I'd planned to go as Mad Max as a joke, and because I could easily borrow the costume from her.

But we didn't dress up for Halloween that night. Mike, Dustin, and I had finally decided we'd outgrown trick-or-treating, and with Will and El gone, Mike wasn't interested in dressing up anyway, so I chose to help Max run away.

We walked the whole way, past all the kids in their bright costumes as they rushed to Loch Nora before all the candy ran out. Max didn't want me to talk her out of it, and I did not try to. By this time, I'd fallen into a place where I was used to her silence and tired of trying to break it. In fact, I went with her because it felt like a rare moment to spend together. And I thought that if she made it to LA and never returned, it would be a fine last night together.

We never made it to the station, though. We got as far as Prospect Avenue before she talked herself out of it, aloud. I watched, silent, as she made the decision, weighing the distance, the money, the dangers of a teenager traveling alone for that long, against the possibility that her dad might not even be there when she arrived. And when she finally decided leaving was a bust, we sat on a nearby bench at the intersection and stared at Halloween decorations in the distance until it was time to go home.

I never told anyone, not because she asked me to keep it a secret but because that was the moment it dawned on me: *Max is not okay.* And I knew, then, that it would only be a matter of time before she unraveled.

We might have broken up, and so many other things have happened since then. But if there's one thing I'm sure I need to do, no matter who I eventually become, it's this—*I need to find my way back to Max.*

Lucas's guide to surviving freshman year:

- ☑ *Make new friends*
- ☑ *Get out of comfort zone and try new things*
- ☑ *~~Be yourself~~ It's okay to be different*
- ☑ *Avoid relationship and friendship drama*
- ☐ *Remember to live in the moment*

PART FOUR

CHAPTER TWENTY-SEVEN

FRIDAY, APRIL 4, 1986

On the day before spring break, I stand in front of my bedroom mirror. I'm not holding two bandanas this time. Instead, I carry two selves, two parts of me in conflict.

The first part of me wants to shove everything and everyone down and throw all focus into the championship game today. The Hawkins Tigers have put blood, sweat, and tears on that court, week in, week out, for the better part of five months. We've made it to the *championship*. Even though I spent all of that time on the bench, watching with bated breath but never getting any playing time, I feel like a part of it all. Now I get to sit there with the rest of the team and witness an opportunity for us to win a state final, the first in over twenty years. If we do, I get to be a part of a championship-winning squad.

There's nothing more dream-come-true than this.

I shouldn't care about whether Mike, Dustin, and Max show up. Mike and Dustin clearly couldn't care less about my basketball career. They haven't shown at any of my games since I've been on varsity.

Call us when you're actually playing, they said. Honestly, they aren't wrong. Doesn't make it any less painful, though.

I keep remembering Jay's words about watching out for myself. Going down this road sure leads to being one with the team, with guys like Jason and Patrick and Andy—a full-time jock, part of the popular gang. It means I'm in dire need of someone to watch my back, just like Jay and I did for each other. I've had no luck making new friends on the team. None like Jay, at least.

Plus, Max is still avoiding me. . . .

I'm stuck here in this middle, unsure which road leads to the devil, and which leads to the angel.

Downstairs, Mom asks me for another photo in my basketball jersey before I leave. Erica, who's gotten one of those OneSteps, takes a picture as well. For the first time, she doesn't laugh at my outfit. If anything's certified cool, it's a varsity uniform—even Erica understands that.

The first part of me wins. No way I'm going to pass up this opportunity just because Mike and Dustin disapprove. But as I leave the house for school, I still can't decide if I've just chosen the right path.

...

The locker room is heated to the top as we prepare for the pep rally. For the first time since the beginning of the season, all of us—starters and benchwarmers both—get to be in the locker room at the same time. At today's pep rally, we're supposed to form a line and make a grand entrance to the gym before Jason gives his speech, which he's now practicing as he paces a corner of the room. I've never seen him this intense, slamming his hand into things when he misses a word or forgets a line. Some of his slams leave dents.

It's a weird feeling, being in here, especially with the upperclassmen present. As usual, I try hard not to look anyone in the eye. Now that Jay is gone—as well as Garroway and the sophomores he hung out with—an oppressive air of silence has settled over the locker room. One where everyone knows what happened, but no one talks about it. But I know some of them still look at me like it was my fault, like I snitched on Garroway to take his spot.

And though no one ever says it, I get the sense that I'm moving up, getting better despite the quiet judgment. Like last week's game against Christian Academy, when Coach almost threw me in as point guard, and a couple of subs gave me hard stares, even though I'm the only point guard left on the team besides Charlie.

I breathe in and out to stem the anxiety. By avoiding those looks, my own gaze somehow ends up falling on Jay's now-vacated locker.

"Missing your old buddy, Sinclair?" asks Andy, slapping me on the shoulder.

"Best get your game face on, freshman," says Patrick. "It's gonna be blood out there on the court today. We're gonna need soldiers."

"Amen to that!" says Andy.

Coach comes in right then. "Look alive, boys. It's time." To Jason, he says: "Ready, Carver?"

Jason looks up from his speech notes with a nod, his hair bouncing. He squeezes the paper into a ball and tosses it into a nearby can, then puts out his hand. "Go Tigers on three." We lean forward. "One, two, three—go Tigers!"

. . .

"And now please welcome the Hawkins High School Tigers!"

The bleachers are packed. I've never worn the uniform before such a loud and vociferous crowd. Hawkins has pulled out the stops in a way I've never experienced: Marching Band in full uniform, everyone else in school colors, the cheer squad performing their latest routines, good old Tiger mascot in an upbeat mood. I haven't yet come to terms with the reality that they're all here for us— *for me!*

The starting upperclassmen race out first, accepting the adulation of the crowd with a practiced ease. Jason in particular is pumped, jumping up and down. I wonder how much of it is just pure euphoria and how much of it is a buzz fueled by something else.

We, the underclassmen, show up at the end of the line. Before I was a player, I'd never come to any of these games. But as I emerge onto the court, the lights seem to shine brighter. I'm sure we look glorious from the bleachers.

Jason grabs the mic from the stand. "Good mooorning, Hawkins Hiiigh!"

The crowd responds with similar energy. There are shrieks of support from girls in the bleachers. I wonder if anyone will ever shriek like that for me. Someday, maybe.

Jason starts his speech, and I notice then that Mike, Dustin, and Max are seated together up there. Staring at me.

I never in a million years thought I'd see them together at the pep rally. For a quick moment, I wonder if they're here to finally support me after all. Then I remember that pep rally attendance is mandatory.

Anyway, better they're here than not. Especially Max, who I'm most glad will finally see me on the court, in uniform. So glad, in fact, that I forget everything that's happened between us and find myself waving at her.

She does not wave back.

Jason gets to the part of the speech where he invokes the Starcourt tragedy for some cheap audience reactions. I watch as Max flinches at mentions of Billy. Even when

Jason mentions Hopper, I feel the part of myself that knows the real story steel. But that moment's soon gone when Jason rouses the crowd with one last hurrah.

"We embarrassed those candy-asses in their own house!" he screams. "And tonight—*tonight!*—we're gonna bring home that championship trophy!"

The bleachers go wild. We share high fives, all of us, starters and subs alike. When I look back to where my friends are sitting in the bleachers, I notice that they're the only ones not celebrating. Mike gives me a deathly stare. For the life of me, I have absolutely no idea why.

CHAPTER TWENTY-EIGHT

FRIDAY, APRIL 4, 1986

"You've got to be kidding me," says Mike.

We are following the throng of students back to class now that the pep rally is over. Between leaving the gym for the locker room and changing back into my regular clothes, I managed to deduce why Mike was so upset when the championship game was announced for tonight.

Today is *also* the final day of the Cult of Vecna campaign. And since I'm technically half a part of Hellfire now, I should be there. Except, I can't. Won't.

It was no surprise, then, that when I stepped out of the locker room, there Mike and Dustin—sans Max—were, waiting for me.

"No, *Eddie* must be kidding," I shoot back as we walk back to class. "I know D&D's fun and whatnot, but are you for real? *Everyone* knows we've been gunning for the championship all season. *Everyone* knows we've got one last game to secure the championship. *Everyone* knew that game was *to-day.* Everyone but Mr. Long Hair, it seems." I shake my head. "You better get him to postpone."

"Again, Lucas," says Dustin, "you've got to be kidding. We can't *postpone* the Cult of Vecna."

"So lemme get this right—you're saying you want me to miss the game and come to Hellfire tonight, but you're *also* saying you would not even consider missing Hellfire to attend *my* game? The *one* time I'm first in line for point guard sub and may actually get a chance to play in a game in front of the school? A *championship* game?"

Mike and Dustin look at one another sheepishly. They know I've made a good point.

We head outside, toward the hallway.

"I don't get the big deal—just talk to Eddie, get him to move Hellfire to another night—"

Dustin scoffs. " 'Just talk to Eddie.' "

"Why don't *you* 'just talk' to your coach, get *him* to move the game?"

"That's a great idea, Mike," Dustin chips in.

I shoot them both looks. "This is the *championship game.*"

"And this is the end of Eddie's campaign!" says Dustin. "A semester of adventuring has led us to this moment. We *need* you."

"And the Tigers don't," says Mike. "No offense, but you haven't come off the bench all season—"

"That's not the point," I say. Didn't they hear what I just said? I'm first in line for point guard sub. There's a *huge* chance I get to step onto that court in this game, even for a few seconds. Would they give up such an opportunity for a random night with Mr. Always Stoned?

We enter the hallway, cutting through the sea of students.

"Listen," I say. "If I get in good with these guys, I'll be in the popular crowd." How does this not register with them? "And then you guys will be too."

"Did it ever cross your mind that maybe we don't *want* to be popular?" asks Mike.

"So you want to be stuck with the nerds and the freaks for three more years?" I like D&D, sure, but not if I have to constantly be associated with Eddie and Gareth and the others who are actually, truly freaks.

"We *are* nerds and freaks," says Dustin.

"Yeah, but maybe we don't have to be."

How can they not see it? They can be anything they want, just like me. They, too, can love D&D *and* basketball *and* hang out with the cool kids if they want. But somehow they want *me* to give up stuff to fit into their boxes? *No.* I refuse to be defined by their one view of the world.

We arrive at Mr. Lansdale's class. I stop and turn to them before going in.

"I'm just—tired." It's hard for me to tell them this difficult truth, but I swallow my pride and let it come out.

"Tired of being bullied, tired of girls laughing at us, tired of feeling like a—a loser. I mean, we came into high school wanting things to be different, right?"

My friends share a look.

"Now we have that chance. I skip tonight, that's *all* out the window." Especially if I get to go out on that court tonight, partake in a championship game. And if we win it, get a championship medal, hold that trophy, show up in the first official championship squad photo in over twenty years. I'll be popular *forever.* And then there'll be no more bombs in my locker.

"So I'm asking you guys, *as a friend*—just get Eddie to move Hellfire and come to my game. *Please.*"

Mike and Dustin share another look.

The bell rings for first period, and I push Mr. Lansdale's door open and go in, hoping that I've finally managed to convince them, for real, that coming to tonight's game is worth it.

Now, for the hard part—convincing Max.

■ ■ ■

The next time I see Max is after first period. I stop Andy and Patrick in the hallway to ask them for some tips on how to prepare for the game. They say stuff like, *Just practice your free throws,* which is great but not particularly groundbreaking. I wonder what today would be like if Jay had stayed.

Max walks by on her way to another class. As usual, she

has her head down, Walkman earphones pulled over her head.

"Hey—" I say in her direction, but she doesn't hear me, zipping past quicker than a speedboat. It's as if she can't wait to get out of the hallways and back into the nowhere she always goes between the times I see her.

"Still not getting any, Sinclair?" asks Andy, and he and Patrick giggle.

"Better make a big move, bro," says Patrick. "Chicks dig big moves."

This may just be the best piece of advice I've received from these two, even if they clearly have offered it unwittingly. Maybe a big kinda move will get Max to listen to me. Giving her tickets to the game will show how much I want her to be there, but . . . what if we win and I'm allowed to carry the trophy and I let her hold it too? It can even be a sweet surprise! But first—tickets. I reach into my backpack and pull out one of the free tickets I've been given as a team member to invite friends and family to the game. I wonder if I can catch her in English.

I look up just in time to see her turn. Not toward English, though, which strikes me as odd. Toward Ms. Kelley's office.

Counseling? I knew she was having trouble, but I never thought it was to the point where she'd get called in for counseling. That was only for students who were flunking or involved in some really bad stuff, like boys who were caught with drugs and girls who got pregnant.

I know Max is no flunker, though, so something is *definitely* up with her. I've noticed that her mood has been dark for a few days now, eyes puffier than usual. That can't be just because she's unhappy with me, or because she's ashamed more people now know that she lives in a trailer park. I need to find out what's eating her. Especially if I'm going to convince her to come to what may be the biggest game of my life.

Seems English will have to wait just a bit longer.

■ ■ ■

I wait for Max outside the counseling office. She doesn't take long, which is a breath of fresh air because it tells me that whatever's up must be less dire than I thought. I still know something is wrong, though, because she looks like absolute shit—hair wild, eyes red like she's taken something, even though I know Max would never.

"Hey, Max—"

She gives me a startled look, then an irritated one. *Can I catch a break?* Then she starts to hurry down the hall, away from me. I have to run to keep pace with her.

"What, are you stalking me or something?"

"No, I just—" I pull out the ticket. "Wanted to give you . . ."

She takes it and peers at it. "What is this?"

"A ticket to the game. . . ."

She shoots me a look that tells me this is *not* the big

gesture I thought it would be. Too late. I consider how I might salvage the five seconds I have left before she obliterates me with her gaze.

"I know you never want to go to my games," I say, opting for the soft touch I applied with Mike and Dustin earlier. If it worked for them, maybe it'll work for her? "But this one is kinda a big deal—"

"*A big deal*," she repeats, cutting me off. "Lucas, you *seriously* care about this?"

"Yeah, I do." Why is everyone acting as though it's wrong to care about something new, or to care about more than one thing at once? "You know—maybe you should find something you care about too. . . ."

Her eyes narrow even further. "What is *that* supposed to mean?" Now I'm, like, two seconds from obliteration. I throw the salvaging course of action out the window and go for what I think is the best possible thing: the truth.

"You're just—not even here anymore," I say. "It's like you're a ghost or something. . . ."

"A ghost?" One second from obliteration. "Really?"

"Max, I know something is wrong." She needs to understand that I care about her, too, and not just this game. She needs to see that I can care about her *and* care about the game.

"Right," she says. "Something must be wrong because I broke up with you."

What? "That's not what I meant—"

"People just . . . change, Lucas. Okay? I've changed.

It's *that simple.*" She pushes the ticket back into my hand. "Good luck."

Before I can respond, she ducks into the girls' bathroom.

I stand there, words caught in my mouth. That is exactly what I've been trying to tell everyone who will listen about change. That I *do* understand it must happen, and it's not a bad thing, and I'm not afraid of it anymore. And even though sometimes it makes me look like I'm the bad guy, the enemy, it just means I'm . . . changing.

This is what I want to tell her: that I understand that *she* is changing, that we're *all* changing. And I can understand and respect that, and even give her room to change if she needs to. What I hope to happen is for her not to be alone—not to have to go through the isolation I've felt all this time. Not to have to live in the upside down much longer. I want to tell her that I'm here to help ease her back to the real world, just as other people have helped me do the same.

But the door of the girls' bathroom stands between us like a mountain, one that I may never be able to climb over to reach her on the other side.

CHAPTER
TWENTY-NINE

FRIDAY, APRIL 4, 1986

I thought the rest of the day would be the absolute best. I was wrong.

At lunch, I sit with the basketball team. I've often sat elsewhere, mostly with Mike and Dustin, sometimes on my own. But *never* at the freak table with Eddie Munson and Gareth and Jeff and the rest. Not even the times when I've been knee-deep in the Vecna campaign with them. But sitting at the jock table today is not really optional. Jason called us all in to talk us through some tips on how to prepare mentally for the game. I don't typically get to sit through these sessions because only the starters do— the rest of us just get team spirit speeches before the game from Coach, like everyone else. But this is a championship game, and Jason thinks it's worthwhile to include even the subs in his captain talks, especially first-in-line subs like me. I wouldn't miss it for anything.

Jason launches into some talk about the game plan. It feels like a D&D huddle, heads put together, trying to solve a problem. Exactly what I've been trying to tell Mike and Dustin: it's not just balls in baskets and assholes in jackets. There's some good stuff in there, and they'd see that if they opened their minds up just a little bit.

The huddle's all going well until Mr. Metal himself, Eddie Munson, hops onto a chair and points at us, saying something aloud that we don't catch. Jason spots him out of the corner of his eye and growls, distracted.

"You want something, freak?" he yells at Eddie.

Eddie sticks out his tongue at us, then makes horns at the sides of his head with his fingers. The boys at the table recoil, disgusted. I duck my head and pray I'm invisible. I've only just been accepted back into this fold. Sorry, Eddie and friends, I'm not going out on a limb for you anytime soon.

"That idiot Munson," says Jason. "One day, I'll drive up to that trailer park of his and just—" He punches his palm and pantomimes smashing Eddie's face. The boys laugh. I don't. I still remember the dents he made in the locker room.

"Don't bother," says Andy. "All you'll do is smell like garbage afterward." The boys chuckle again.

"Not everyone who lives in a trailer park is trash."

The words are out of my mouth before I realize I'm speaking. They don't know that Max lives in the *exact same* trailer park that Eddie does, and to my understanding, she is very much *not trash*.

Jason frowns, zeroes in on me. He hasn't really paid me much attention, not since that first day, and not quite as much since my return and promotion.

"You say something, Sinclair?"

I shake my head. "It was just—nothing. Never mind."

"Oh, I *do* mind," he says. "I do mind that a nonstarting freshman, who only got to pass tryouts because of Jermaine Demario, thinks we want to hear his opinions on trailer parks." He leans forward. "You think because you got a sophomore's spot, it means you can say whatever you want? You think you're Jay now?"

"I don't—"

"Shh, shh," Patrick says, placing a hand on mine. "Captain's still speaking."

Jason shakes his head. "This is a *championship game*, Sinclair. Odds are your butt sticks to that bench until the buzzer, so you're really only here because Coach insists. Until you go out there and prove yourself, don't think you can just leech off us who do all the work, and spend all your time defending trailer parks."

He picks up where he left off with the game talk, but I'm no longer listening. My mind drifts away, thinking about Jay, realizing now the difficulty of the choices he had to make all along. What once seemed to me like a weak reason to leave Hawkins—struggling to be accepted—starts to make sense. It wasn't just struggling to fit into two places that was the problem: it was struggling to be *accepted* by both. Yet again, he was right. There's no winning. The only way to win would be to choose.

I look back to the freak table, where Eddie Munson throws a newspaper to Mike and Dustin. They scurry out of the cafeteria right after. I wonder what task he's sent them off to do and whether they've succeeded in getting him to postpone tonight's Hellfire. Whether they'll finally be able to make it to the game.

...

After school, there's not much time left to prepare for the game. I consider returning home to do some shooting practice before heading back to the gym again. But once Mom drops me off at home—she insisted—I don't even bother going inside. I pick up my bike and ride out, screaming something probably inaudible to a perplexed Mom about going to the neighborhood court.

As I ride, breezing past the sidewalks and hedges, hoping the sickly-sweet smell of wet flowers in the spring air will calm my nerves, I can't shake the feeling that *something* is going to happen today. Whether that thing is good or bad remains to be seen, but I feel it already. Today is a day for Big Happenings.

Maybe it's because I'm feeling less confident that my friends will show up. I heard some chatter in study hall that Mike and Dustin were going about trying to get someone to join their group for the last Hellfire campaign tonight. I was sure the study hall kids were mistaken—Mike and Dustin were coming to my game, obviously. Maybe Eddie didn't postpone and they had to go out and look for replacements—for me and then for themselves, since they would be at the game.

But as I ride on, I realize I can't be so sure anymore. My last rule for survival—*remember to live in the moment*—includes embracing all change, whatever form it comes in. If my friends think my games and feelings and interests no longer matter, then so be it. If they've become selfish pricks who are too invested in the characters of a made-up game to care about the actual human friend they have, then there's little I can do about that. I've done my best and shown up for them this whole time.

As Jay said, friends need to earn that title. If Mike and Dustin choose not to show up for me tonight, I may have to start looking for some new friends.

When I get to the court, it's empty, which means I can practice some shooting if I want to. But I didn't bring my ball. It dawns on me now that most of the times Jay helped me with practice here, it was his ball we used.

Jay's absence falls on me like a bucket of water, a person-shaped hole in my life. I have to put my bike down and sit on a nearby bench, a weight on my chest I can't explain.

I've had a small taste of what it means to lose a friend before—for a while, we all thought Will was dead and gone. But this is different. Things have been moving so fast that I never really made space to think about what it means to lose someone who understands me on a different level. Sure, Max understands me like that, too, but hanging out with Jay offered me the freedom to say out loud all the stuff I've never said before.

Which is why no one who isn't Jermaine—a Black basketball kid in Hawkins who defies expectations—can fill that space. But I'm the new Black basketball kid in Hawkins now. And if the mold for who I must be should be broken, then I have to go out there and break it. I have to be Lucas Sinclair: irregular, different, unlimited.

The rubbery bounce of a ball on hard court jerks me back to the present. Some of the neighborhood boys have shown up to play. I don't bother to wait and see if they'll make any trouble. I pick up my bag and leave.

On my ride back, I'm less nervous, maybe even de-termined. To *show them.* To show everyone that *I contain multitudes,* that there's more to the new Black kid on the team, and not just because Coach thinks any Black kid *has* to be on the team. I'm also the Black kid who loves horror movies and *Karate Kid* and "satanic" D&D; who is Hawkins through and through—born, bred, bled for; who cares about his ex-girlfriend who lives in a trailer park; who has fought monsters *three times* and saved a town that doesn't even acknowledge he's there. No more hiding, no more apologizing, no more waiting for some other time to be myself. The time is now, and I'm ready, wholly and unashamedly.

I'm ready to live in the moment.

I pedal fast back to the gym, only one thought on my mind: *The real Lucas is coming, and Hawkins had better get ready.*

CHAPTER THIRTY

FRIDAY, APRIL 4, 1986

Everything before game time is a blur. Ordinarily, I'd be either stuck by the lockers, uninterested, or seated at the back with the other subs, struggling to keep pace with Coach's tactics. Today is better. Because of Jason's little huddle at lunch, not much of what Coach says is new to me, though it isn't any more understandable.

Strategy and ball talk whiz over my head, in and out of my ears. I know it's important stuff, but I've made a habit of not listening, because I never get subbed in anyway. Besides, if I get subbed in today, I'm pretty sure I'll be told exactly what to do. What I've learned so far is that the most important thing is for me to go out there and play my heart. Even with something I'm not really that great at—like basketball—the key to success remains the same: *being myself.*

After giving us pointers on what to watch out for in their best players, Coach encourages us not to dwell on the team's name, to purge it from memory.

"Today, they are a nameless, faceless opponent." Spit flies out of his mouth as he speaks. "All I want you to see are opposition colors, a crowd of bodies to be barged through on our way to the championship. I want you to ram through those bodies. I want you to go out there and play until your joints ache, your eyes water, your knees bleed. Your blood, sweat, and tears—that's what I want to see out on that court."

I'm sure every other teammate is going out there to play for the championship, but not me. At least not primarily. If I get to display my blood, sweat, and tears, it will be for me. I'm going out there to choose myself, to embrace all my faults and weaknesses, to fearlessly show the real Lucas Sinclair to the world.

. . .

After tactics talk, it's time to take the court.

The away team goes out first. The boos are louder than the cheers, which tells me we have a bigger crowd than usual.

Deafening noise greets us when we pour out onto the court. The cheer squad is going hard, the band at full volume, the bleachers overflowing. I thought the pep rally was the peak of my time on this team, but I was wrong. Even if I don't set my foot on that court, even if we don't win this championship, this will likely be one of the greatest nights of my life.

We rise for the national anthem. Our singer is a bright and lively Nashville transplant named Tammy Thompson, who, it turns out, used to go here. *Returning to Hawkins? That's a first.* As soon as she starts singing, though, it becomes clear why she's back so soon. I poke a finger in my ear to feign taking out wax.

With the lights pointing down on the court and into my eyes, it's hard to see the bleachers well, especially as packed as they are. But something in me already knows my friends aren't here.

My chest tightens. I want to be sad, angry, maybe even vengeful. But instead, I'm just disappointed. Half because they won't get to see me on the slim chance that I play on the biggest stage of my life; the other half because they don't get to see me . . . *become.*

When the anthem is over, I take my seat on the bench, the ball is tossed, and the game begins.

■ ■ ■

If I'm asked later how this game went until the last quarter, I won't know, because I spend the first three quarters in two minds.

First: I was lying to myself when I said I wasn't pissed at my friends. I'm royally incensed.

Second: the Tigers aren't doing as well as planned. Which means whatever dreams I had about being subbed into the game—gone.

We take the lead pretty quickly, running up twenty-six points in no time. In my head, the Tigers are poised to crush the opposition. But they soon counter and go past us. By the end of the first quarter, they're three points ahead. Coach is furious.

"Did you not hear anything I said in that room?" he bellows during the first-quarter break. "Go out there and guard your man!"

The second quarter goes by kind of the same way. We catch up, but every time we make a shot, they find their way back in. Every little hope of joy, of winning, of things working out as planned, gets cut off before we can even celebrate it.

I find myself glancing at the bleachers. *Maybe they're just late,* I think. *Maybe they were caught up with something. Maybe there's an emergency and I don't know. Maybe Will and El are back! Or the Russians? Maybe there's a new monster in Hawkins?*

But just like the opposition's shots, each question is answered with the truth: my friends are not here, on my biggest day of all, because they don't think my game is that important. They don't think *I'm* that important. They don't think I'm friend enough.

By the third quarter, it's clear that we're going to lose unless something drastic happens. And the moment I think that, it happens.

The opposing captain, a tall and mean center with a ruthless fouling streak, crashes into Charlie just as he's going for a layup. Jason gets up in the center's face, veins crisscrossing his forehead, and the refs have to call for a bit of calm. I've been watching Charlie the whole game. Something's been a bit off with him—he's distracted, dallying on the ball, traveling.

We win a free throw from that misfortune, but more misfortune follows. Charlie can't stand. He has to be helped up by teammates, and soon he's limping toward the bench. I'm so caught up in the ruckus that I don't even hear my name.

"Sinclair!"

I look up at the voice, surprised. Coach.

"You're in!" he says.

My eyes widen. "Wha—"

"You're in! Let's go!"

I take off my overshirt and pants in a daze. This is it. The moment I've been waiting for. This is my chance. My head turns involuntarily toward the bleachers to catch the gaze of someone I know and understand, someone whose eyes say: *Yes, you did it. Go on and give them hell.* There are no such eyes in the stands, though. No friends.

But what I do see are hundreds of people waiting to see me. The *real* me. Whatever they once knew about me, they're no longer interested in. The only thing they will see and remember for years to come is what I put before them on this court, on the biggest stage of all.

Breathe, I can hear Jay's voice telling me, like in our practice sessions. *Just breathe.*

I shut my eyes, breathe, and get ready to take on the world.

• • •

My job is simple. I only have to do three things: defend, pass to Jason, shoot if open. Of course, there are more things I should be doing as a point guard—Charlie takes most of the team's layups, for instance. But Coach is worried that we're susceptible to fast breaks and wants me to contribute my tenacity and fresh legs to defense.

I spend most of the remaining quarter defending, warding off attacks, and passing to Jason or the wing when he's not open. I prime my ear to filter out every sound but two: Coach's and Jason's voices, parsing their instructions, translating them into hands and feet and off-the-ball movement.

Each time I find my hands shaking, palms sweaty, the sound of the crowd getting too loud, anxiety threatening to choke me, I remember why I'm playing. *Not just for the championship, Lucas.* I'm playing because I never want to be bullied anymore, never want people to look at me and see someone in whose locker a bomb trap can be set. I'm playing because I want people to look at me and *see* me. I'm playing for Jay, and Max, and Mike, and Dustin—even though I'm completely pissed at most of them right now.

I'm playing for everyone like us: so that we may all exist in this town and be ourselves, unashamed, unafraid, unlimited.

At 68–69, with ten seconds on the clock, and the Tigers down by a point, everything changes.

It starts with Jason calling a time-out. Coach gives instructions for our last play, with Jason insisting on the same point: *Everyone, pass the ball to me.* But he's our primary scorer, the best shooter left on the court—there's no way he won't be mobbed in the last ten seconds. Coach thinks so, too, and makes it known. But for some reason, Jason insists that he can do it.

Still, I make a mental note to position myself just right in case of any rebound opportunities.

Whistle blows, game resumes. I clean the dripping sweat from my face as play starts. The ball goes to Jason, and immediately, as predicted, he's swarmed.

He tries his best, I'll give that to him. A fancy fake-out here, some footwork there, and he manages to break the ankles of two defenders.

He shoots.

He misses.

Hands reach forward for the rebound, including mine.

The only thought in my head is, *God, let a Tiger pick this up!* But then, somehow, the ball is in my hands, and I'm looking at it, and I realize that I'm the Tiger on the rebound.

Shoot! comes the scream from the crowd. Or maybe it's in my head.

The nearest defender advances toward me.

Eyes on the court, Jay says in my head. *We don't have to be the best all the time. We just have to be enough for ourselves.*

I open up my body, step aside, evade the defender's lunge. The player goes one way, giving me just enough space to shoot.

Two seconds on the clock.

Be enough for yourself, says Jay. *Everything else is secondary.*

I jump. I shoot.

I don't know exactly what happens after that. I don't even see the shot go in. I don't hear the buzzer. All I hear is the bleachers change from collective held breath to wild ecstasy, and then a deafening roar of victory.

A crowd of people swallows me up—coaches, teammates, medics. A smile plants itself on my face and won't let up. The crowd presses in, tighter, tighter, everyone reaching for me in celebration and congratulations. It is more than everything I could've wished for. I look from face to face to face and see respect, adulation, maybe even love.

So why have I never felt so . . . alone?

CHAPTER THIRTY-ONE

FRIDAY, APRIL 4, 1986

We burst into the locker room, and I'm riding high on my teammates' shoulders. They accidentally bang my head against the doorframe, but I'm not even upset.

Once the guys put me down, they take turns pouring cans of Jolt Cola over my head. Tradition, for the team's MVP and winner, they say. For once I'm glad I'm not in my nice clothes, though getting this out of my hair will be another matter. I also wonder what the janitors will think, and I tell my teammates so, but they laugh even harder.

"Ah, Sinclair," says Jason. "Still living in the regular world, are you? You don't have to anymore, remember?

You're one of us now. And we don't play by the rules out there."

He's right, I think. I've finally found my place. Even if it's in a sport I never thought I'd play, and among guys I never thought I'd want to be around. But it wasn't always about the game or these guys. It was always about living in the moment, about being as comfortable here with myself as I am anywhere else and with anything else. I have no reason to feel any shame for enjoying the benefits that come with hanging out with cool jocks. Especially if my own friends have chosen to forsake me altogether.

"Listen, we could even do one better," says Jason, emptying a last can of Jolt Cola and crushing it. "But Coach's a stickler and makes a big deal about the stink after." He pauses. "Lemme guess. You haven't had your first taste of a real man's drink yet."

My face shows my alarm. "You mean . . . alcohol?"

"Alcohol—" Jason chuckles, turns to the team. "Gentlemen, he calls it alcohol!"

The boys laugh, and Jason returns to me.

"I'm talking *beers,* Sinclair. Now that you've become a real man tonight, you need a real man's drink. And if you're yet to have your first taste—well, we'll fix that, won't we, boys?"

The team cheers their agreement. Some part of me wants to say, *Won't we get in trouble for drinking?* But the other part of me, the one that wants to continue sticking it to the world, says, *I am Lucas Sinclair. And I can be and do whatever the hell I want.*

Coach comes in later and gives his own rousing speech, talking about what our victory means for the team, the school, the town, his own athletic legacy. He has a small word of praise for me, but otherwise, it's back to celebration.

We hit the showers right after and change into regular clothes. Andy and Patrick argue about whether the Hideaway will let the team and other high schoolers in for a celebration.

"They will if they don't want to become social pariahs," says Andy. "Imagine being the bar that won't let a town celebrate their first championship in over twenty years."

"They're not keeping the town out," says Patrick. "Just us. Chief Powell doesn't play fast and loose like Hopper, remember? He won't take kindly to them letting us in."

"Well, we've gotta party somewhere, don't we?" says Andy, looking to Jason. "Ideas, Cap?"

Jason nods sagely, as if he's been waiting for this very question to be asked.

"Word on the street," he says, "is that a certain someone—aka me—has made plans to turn the old abandoned Benny's into a fun house for the '86 champs. How's that sound, fellas?"

Hoots and cheers go around the room. Andy, who has made a boom box materialize from nowhere, turns it up. The boys jump some more to "Rhythm of the Night," dancing and clapping in a circle. It doesn't take long for them to pull me in, a shoe in one hand, the other on my foot. I dance anyway, carefree.

After the song, they turn to the news as we finish up. The media is still talking about us, the Hawkins Tigers. And what do you know—they mention my name! Not just my name, but also how I've been on the bench all season, yet came on in the final to win it for the team. *A nobody*, they say. *Now somebody.*

I hold my head just a little bit higher as we leave the locker room. Jason goes off to find his girlfriend, Chrissy, while everyone else heads out to Benny's Burgers. There are still some students, a few staff, and parents milling about in the parking lot. They give us back pats, high fives, and hugs when we go by. I'm reminded again of how none of these come from my friends, how they're not even here to join in my euphoria. Until, that is, a freshman from the cheer squad stops in front of me and smiles.

"Nice going," she says.

It takes me a moment to realize she's addressing me.

"Th-thanks?"

"No, thank *you*," she says. "You just made all those grueling hours on our cheer routines worth it."

I gulp.

"I'm Becca," she says. "But you must know me from cheer squad."

"Yes, yes," I say, even though I have absolutely no idea who she is.

"You're gonna come by Benny's Burgers, right?" she says, preparing to get in a car with two other girls.

"Uhh—"

"Course he is!" says Jason, materializing out of nowhere to wrap an arm around my shoulder. "The Tigers' new star won't miss it for the world. I'll deliver him there myself."

Becca tilts her head toward the car. "Chrissy joining us?"

"Yeah, she's gonna be a while," he says. "Had to go home to get changed or something."

"Okey-doke. See you boys there." She turns her attention back to me. "I'll be looking out for you, star." She gives me a wink and then gets in, and the car speeds off.

"Ooh, tonight's about to be your night in more ways than one, Sinclair," says Patrick as Jason leads us to his car. They banter and tease me about it, but I can't hear them through all the beaming.

Star, she called me. For the first time in forever, I feel *seen.*

Just as we approach the car, though, the smile vanishes from my face.

Also leaving the parking lot, oblivious to my death stare, are Mike and Dustin and . . . *Erica?* She's supposed to be covering for me at home, like we agreed. *I'm supposed to be sleeping over at Mike's!* They're all dressed in Hellfire shirts, which means they must have gone on to hold the campaign after all. Also, is Erica carrying an American flag? *Jesus, this kid.*

I can't process what my eyes are seeing. *They were here the whole time? And chose Eddie Munson and Freak United over me?*

I'm so confused by the sight of them that I stand frozen for a bit, once again caught between these two worlds of mine. My chest tightens. Hurt and anger rise to my throat, and I swallow both down.

"Sinclair!" calls Jason. "You coming?"

The Lucas Sinclair of old would have let himself get caught up in all of this. He would've let himself get carried away in the *why* of it, trying to make sense of how the only friends he's known since childhood decided to forsake him, choosing themselves over his feelings and leaving him to face his challenges alone. They told him, without saying the words, that they have chosen their path, and it is his turn to choose his. They have embraced their change, and it is time for him to do the same.

"Coming, Sinclair?"

I tear my gaze away, unafraid. The new Lucas Sinclair understands that change sometimes means losing friends, and taking a different road, and understanding that life will turn out different for everyone, and that's just fine. This Lucas Sinclair will no longer put his time and energy into things and people of old that add no value to his life. This Lucas Sinclair will not feel any guilt and will embrace the bright future that now presents itself before him.

This Lucas Sinclair is *done*.

"Sinclair!"

"Coming," I say, and turn away.

Lucas's guide to surviving freshman year:

- ☑ *Make new friends*
- ☑ *Get out of comfort zone and try new things*
- ☑ *~~Be yourself~~ It's okay to be different*
- ☑ *Avoid relationship and friendship drama*
- ☑ *Remember to live in the moment*
- ☐ *Help my friends*

PART FIVE

CHAPTER
THIRTY-TWO

SATURDAY, APRIL 5, 1986

I wake up to morning light filtering through the window. There's a banging in my head and my tongue is rough and feels too big for my mouth. Also, something tastes bitter, like I chewed pills or something. Or drugs?

Oh, shit. I think back to the party, trying to remember what happened. I get flashes of different short memories: spray-painting TIGERS FOREVER! and '86 CHAMPS on the boarded-up windows outside; the cheerleader girl, Becca, laughing at my jokes, running a finger down my arm; dancing to "The Sweetest Taboo" with her; drinking games, chugging a lot of beer; another drinking game; a third drinking game; lots and lots of drinking.

Whew, no drugs. I sit up, and my head spins. It takes me a while to right myself, and when I do, I realize I'm on an unfamiliar couch. I look around, stunned.

I'm still at Benny's.

Colorful lights, now unlit, hang from the ceiling. Beer kegs from last night are strewn around, orbited by discarded empty beer bottles, red cups, and half-eaten food. Nearby, someone—I can't make out who—is passed out on the floor, shirtless, with a mustache drawn on his face.

I run a hand over my head. I hope Erica ended up getting home early enough to cover for me. Hopefully, my parents still think I stayed over at Mike's and don't call the Wheelers before I get home.

I'm thinking all this when my vision swirls and my stomach contracts. A wave of nausea comes over me, and my belly prepares to give up its contents. I dash for the bathroom, brushing past a bunch of others who slept here after the party, and through the bathroom door, where I chuck my head into the toilet bowl and spill all my guts.

The banging in my head intensifies, now accompanied by a constant ringing in my ears. The edges of my vision remain fuzzy. The yellow liquid in the toilet bowl, the aftertaste in the back of my throat, and the heartburn clawing at my chest tell me I definitely had one too many beers, but for the life of me, I can't even remember the taste.

It takes me a while to notice that the continued banging is not coming from my head, but from someone knocking on the bathroom door. It opens, and Jason is standing there with a smirk, eating straight from a box of cereal.

"You all right in there, Sinclair?"

"Yeah," I say between spittle. "I'm good."

He says something about first hangovers as he leaves, but I don't hear because I'm trying to get my brain back. I sit and lean my head on the wall.

The darker parts of last night come trickling in. The high of the celebration quickly dampened by seeing Mike and Dustin walk away with Erica. Now that I've had the time, I have some words ready for those two (not Erica, since she's covering for me). But I'm not going to get to that, because it's spring break, and Mike must have already left to visit El and Will on that Lenora Hills trip he planned a while back. Dustin will spend spring break as he spends most holidays—talking to Suzie all day. My words will have to wait.

Maybe that's for the best, because with my headache finally subsiding, some clarity begins to arrive. Last night was great—no doubt. Making the championship-winning shot was epic. Hearing my name over the speakers, on the radio, on the lips of everyone at school—that, I'll never forget. Party was a blast, too. Everyone who's anyone, all in one place. And by the time spring break ends, I get to be one of those people. I get to be *someone*.

Yet something still feels . . . incomplete.

I've never been this angry with my friends. There's also nothing I want more desperately than to have shared these moments of euphoria with them. Now it may be too late, which just makes me angry all over again. I don't care whether we're still a party like before—we're still friends, and friends care about each other. The *one* time I wanted them to care—that I *asked* them to—they refused. That's messed up.

There's some chatter going on in the main dining area, where the rest of the team who stayed over are gathering. I can hear their lazy hungover voices arguing over the voices on the small TV they're watching. For a moment, I think it's the *ThunderCats* Andy had said they were going to watch this morning, until I listen closer and realize it's the news.

Ugh, yet another report about the devil in Hawkins, I think, but then something else catches my attention. It's the sound of cars approaching the building. But at the same time, a string of words from the report filters into my ears.

Murder . . . actively investigating . . . this trailer behind me . . .

I shoot to my feet, jerked back to reality, the hangover cleared completely from my eyes and only one word on my mind.

Max.

I fly out of the toilet, stepping over the passed-out body again. A couple of the boys are at the window, peering outside, while the rest rush to tuck away as much of the scene as they can.

Outside, Chief Powell and Officer Callahan are walking up to the door.

...

It all happens so fast. One minute, we're looking at a TV reporter talk about a Hawkins student getting murdered at the trailer park in Forest Hills—*Max's* trailer park. Next thing we know, the police boot us out back. Everyone but Jason.

When Chief Powell knocked on the door and ordered us outside, I was a hundred percent sure they were here for me. Even though most of the boys thought they'd come on a noise complaint, I knew for sure that this had something to do with that murder in East Hawkins. So I braced for the news.

But they asked for Jason instead. Now I'm confused, but no less freaked-out. Maybe they want to speak to us about the party. They could definitely bring us all in for underage drinking. *Then* Dad will be vindicated in asking me if I was sure I wanted to be hanging out with "those jokers." That's after he's had his fill of berating my head off.

That's not what most scares me, though. I'm thinking about Max—she could still be in danger, for all I know. Eddie Munson's the only other Hawkins High student I know who lives in that park, so maybe once I leave here, I can find someone from Hellfire and get them to track Munson. Maybe he'll know what happened.

Patrick tries to calm me down, reminding me it could just be a noise complaint. But I know better. The feeling I had from yesterday's bike ride returns. Goose bumps spread over my arms and neck.

Something's wrong with Hawkins. *Again.*

I'm thinking this when Jason bursts out the back door, dazed. His eyes are unfocused, and he stumbles forward. He looks like he's just seen a ghost.

"Jason—dude," says Patrick. "You all right?"

"What's going on?" I ask at the same time Andy wants to know if the police are going to contact our parents and report us.

But Jason isn't listening. He walks right past us, straight toward the woods. I share looks with Andy and Patrick, and we silently agree it makes sense to follow him.

We trail Jason only a couple of yards before he drops to the ground, on his knees, right on the edge of the woods. Then he grabs his hair and starts to scream.

■ ■ ■

Chrissy Cunningham, star cheerleader and Jason's girl-friend, is the murdered student.

After the police leave us with a stern warning to clean up and go home, we manage to get Jason to stop crying and come back inside, take a breath, and tell us what he knows. But instead of taking that breath, once he's wiped his eyes, he thrashes through a stack of books abandoned in a corner and fishes out last year's Hawkins High yearbook.

He flips through it, agitated, until he lands on a particular page: Hellfire Club.

My body goes rock solid.

He puts a finger on the person dead center in the club photograph, speaking their name: "Eddie Munson."

I hover a few feet away and try to put it all together as Jason tells the story, the team gathered about him at the table. Apparently, Chrissy went to Eddie Munson's trailer to buy drugs—which Jason finds completely unbelievable—and ended up dead in his trailer. Not just dead. *Mutilated*, from Jason's description. And somehow the police think Eddie Munson's responsible.

The story makes absolutely no sense to me. I've sat with Eddie Munson, played D&D with him. Is he a freak? Absolutely. A jackass? Kinda. But I'm not quite on board with the idea that he's a vicious murderer. Not yet.

Now Andy's talking about Eddie probably sacrificing Chrissy and draining her blood for some satanic ritual, and Jason's talking about Hellfire as if it's some sort of cult. I don't know when I butt into the conversation and stop them in their tracks.

"Hellfire isn't a cult." Now that I've started, I can't stop. "And it has nothing to do with Satan. It's just . . . a D&D club."

The whole table turns to stare at me. Confusion. I quickly try to explain how it's a game, a fantasy, like *Lord of the Rings*. But their stares remain, and I realize that nobody's confused—they're suspicious. Suddenly Andy wants to know how I know so much about Hellfire and "games like that." I quickly find a way to deflect, explaining that Erica plays—only half a truth. This eases them off.

But then Jason carries on, talking about how satanic cults warp people's minds and confuse their realities and cause innocent people to die. He calls it an epidemic happening all over the country. Patrick supports his arguments with something he's read.

Then the conversation swivels suddenly. Jason holds up the photo of Eddie, saying he probably murdered Chrissy because he's being manipulated by a satanic game. Which means—

"He's gonna kill again," Patrick completes the sentence.

"But not if we can help it," says Jason.

And out of nowhere, he begins one of his rousing speeches, pacing back and forth, charging up the boys. He talks about sidestepping the cops and clearing Chrissy's name. He talks about what Chrissy would want him to do: go out there and *hunt some freaks.*

The squad, fired up, roars their approval.

My blood runs cold. I realize now that those slams in the locker room were not just him being on edge before a game. This dude is *bananas.*

Now I'm back to thinking about Max, who lives only a few trailers away. And as much as I'm upset with my friends, I still whisper a prayer for Mike (*please, please, already be on a plane to Lenora Hills*) and Dustin—even Erica.

Everyone who's affiliated with Hellfire is in danger at this moment.

Including me.

Jason rips the Hellfire page from the yearbook, takes out a lighter, and then sets the page on fire. The blackened edges of the page curl around and succumb to the flames. I watch with the building dread that my own life—and the lives of the only friends I have left and still care about—is next.

CHAPTER THIRTY-THREE

SUNDAY, APRIL 6, 1986

The next morning, I wake to the sound of clanking. The noise filtering into my ears comes from outside. The sounds of gathering, voices in agreement. Sounds of planning and preparation, a team getting ready to move out. I rise from the couch, blinking myself alert. Still at Benny's Burgers. Except, my teammates are no longer gathered here in the main dining area, where I last left them before I went to sleep on the couch. They're the source of the noise outside.

I follow the sound.

Yesterday, I somehow brought calm back to the house. I talked—a lot more than I ever have. Reminded them that the Hellfire kids are just teenagers like us all, that they're probably just as scared about the murder and sad about Chrissy as we are. That Eddie Munson, whether he's a Satanist or whatever, is definitely not out there Ted Bundying Hawkins High students. He doesn't even talk to girls! He's a crazy dude, yeah, and maybe even a bit of a freak, but being a weirdo doesn't make someone a murderer.

I managed to get them to cool off for the rest of the day. They spent it watching more reports, and then later getting back to *ThunderCats*. Jason took a nap and woke up feeling better, like all his rage had burned away with that Hellfire photo. We ordered pizza and they had some more beers—I declined.

Once things settled down, I did some thinking of my own, wondering about the source of the uneasiness I'd been feeling all along. Did I enjoy playing basketball with these guys? Yes. Did I enjoy the party, the attention, the flashing lights of popularity? Yes. But the other stuff—like all this *aggression* and this need to force others to accept the way they interpreted the world—*that* I didn't pay enough attention to. I'd been so caught up in being a jock myself that I never considered who I'd become, what kind of company I'd kept. Judging by what went down that afternoon, I wondered: *Will I always have to put out their fires?*

At night, the boys played cards, and I went to bed, wondering yet again if I needed to check in at home now that news of a student murder was going around. But, feeling like I had done a good job of keeping things from exploding, I slept early. *Maybe tomorrow,* I thought, *I'll go home, and then I'll go find Max.*

But as I walk out the door now, I see them.

Jason, Patrick, and Andy are all that's left, tossing some tools into the trunk of Jason's Jeep. My brain says *tools,* but as I look at the actual items they're packing—tire irons, duct tape, crowbars—my mind clocks them for what they really are: *weapons.*

"Well, well," says Andy, spotting me. "Look who's decided to join."

"What are you doing?" I ask.

"Gearing up," says Patrick.

"Preparing for the hunt," Andy adds.

All the dread from yesterday drops back into me. I must have winced at the sudden turn of events because Jason, who's moving stuff with a painfully focused expression, notices my trepidation. He makes an effort to stop, put an arm around my shoulder, and let me know it's all good— they're not going to *kill* Eddie, just ask him to confess his crime. *A friendly neighborhood chat,* as Andy put it. They chuckle, but it's not funny. In this moment, I want nothing more than for the police to find Eddie Munson first. At least he'll be safe from these dudes.

Jason says it's okay if I want to step away—no judgment. But I remember that their search will probably lead them to Forest Hills, to Max. Their quest for Hellfire members might circle back to Dustin. The way they're moving, someone's gonna get hurt, and I can't let that happen—not even to Eddie Munson.

I choose to go with them.

"All right," says Jason, slamming the trunk closed. "Let's capture us a freak."

· · ·

The drive doesn't take long. I'm staring out the window the whole time, trying to get my bearings and paying no attention to Andy and Patrick's argument about why Patrick has a nosebleed. I have no idea where we are or where we're going until I realize we've crossed the railway tracks. And even after I get my sense of direction back and process that we're not headed for the trailer park, I'm not particularly relieved. If we're not headed to Forest Hills, *where* are we going?

Jason, who's way too focused, grips the steering wheel and keeps his eyes on the road, as if trying to bore a hole through the windshield. He does not say a single word.

Not until, out of nowhere, he swerves the Jeep, and we come to a stop in front of a garage.

I'll never know how Jason found this address, but the moment I step out of the car, I see why we're here.

It's Gareth and Jeff from Hellfire, along with two other guys I don't know but I've definitely seen around. They've got a band setup going, and are jamming heavy metal music. The music grinds to a halt when they spot us. Gareth rises, the band name Dirty Scabs on his shirt and spray-painted on the bass drum. He squints, trying to identify us.

"You're a bit early, fellas," he says. "Show's not until next week."

Andy says something mocking the music, but Jason goes straight to the point.

"We're looking for Eddie Munson," he says. "He's in this band—if that's what you can even call this—right?"

Gareth tells him off, then immediately spots me.

"Lucas?" His eyes grow suspicious. "What are you doing with these douchebags?"

I freeze as Jason, Patrick and Andy turn their eyes to me, equally surprised.

"You know these freaks, Sinclair?"

Yes, my mouth wants to say, but the angel and demon on my shoulders hold me back. *No, you don't know them,* one part tells me. *You've met them, what, a couple of times? These are not your friends. Friends have to earn the title. Focus on your* real *friends.*

"They know my sister" is all I say, which is technically true. Erica did play with them during the championship game, didn't she?

But Jason's eyes have not left mine, and it's clear he's going to need more convincing than that.

"They tried to recruit me," I add. "To their club— *cult—*"

"Lucas—what the hell?" says Jeff.

It's too late—the words are already out of my mouth. I

only said that to clarify for Jason—*he's* the one who's been calling Hellfire a cult all along, right? I just want him to know what I'm talking about. I just want them to know that all I care about is finding Eddie. Finding Eddie so Max and Dustin (and Mike, when he comes back) can be safe.

"We—we just need to find Eddie," I say.

"Well, you got eyes, don't you? He's not here—"

Jason cuts Gareth short with a sucker punch to his nose, then grabs and slams him against the garage wall. Jeff and the others move to defend him, but Patrick and Andy are quickly on them, holding them back without effort.

I back up two steps, heart racing. *It's happening.* This is *exactly* what I've been trying to avoid, and now it's happening anyway. My mouth is dry, and I can't form words to tell them to stop.

With Gareth weak and bleeding from his nose, his back against the wall, Jason leans forward, face in face. His preppie look is long gone—Jason is more menacing than I've ever seen him. Crazed, almost. He reminds me of Billy, of the Flayed. All desire, no forethought.

"Where is he?" he asks.

Gareth has no idea. So Jason picks up where he left off and throws Gareth into the drum set, cymbals crashing. Gareth tries to get up, but Jason stomps a foot on his back, keeping him down. Then he steps on Gareth's hand, slowly.

"Gonna be hard to play those drums with a broken hand," he says, pressing harder. Gareth screams as Jason's foot comes down, crushing him to the ground.

I brace for the sound of bones breaking, when—

"Dustin!" says Gareth.

My eyes grow wide. *Dustin?*

"Dustin . . . Henderson," says Gareth, the words rolling out of his mouth fast. "He was . . . calling around, looking for Eddie. Maybe . . . maybe he found him. . . ."

My heart is now fully in my mouth. *Dustin calling around for Eddie?* Not that it sounds far-fetched or anything— Dustin has always been a certified busybody—but why was he looking for Eddie too? Did he know something we didn't?

Then I realize, with a sinking feeling, that Jason has also come to the same conclusion, because he kneels next to Gareth and says:

"Where do we find this Dustin?"

CHAPTER THIRTY-FOUR

SUNDAY, APRIL 6, 1986

I say nothing when Gareth gives Dustin's address to Jason. I say nothing when we all get back in the car. I say nothing on the drive over there, trying to mask my growing panic by staring out the window and avoiding Patrick's and Andy's eyes, or Jason's through the rearview mirror. I say nothing when we arrive at the house and get out of the car.

The only way to protect Dustin right now is to have absolutely nothing to do with him.

Jason knocks on the front door. I already know no one's home—Mrs. Henderson is never home on weekend mornings, and if Dustin's out looking for Eddie, the house must be empty. So while they're preoccupied with knocking, I hang back and wait for the right moment, when their attention is divided.

Then I slip away.

Dustin's room is around the side, and thankfully is not a climb like mine. Getting through the window so quickly is a hassle, and I don't make light work of it, tumbling to the floor. Without waiting to check whether my limbs are still intact, I scramble over to what I'm here for.

Cerebro 2.0.

Outfitting the antenna on his roof, Dustin also made sure to configure walkies to his ham radio. Even though he technically can't talk to Suzie from his walkie while he's out—and thank God he can't, or we'd all be deaf from his bragging—he still carries those walkies everywhere, in case he needs to be reached for emergencies.

Emergencies such as these.

I smash the talk button on the radio rig.

"Dustin, it's Lucas." I feel like we're back in 1983, searching for Will again. "Do you copy?"

A crackle. Then: "Lucas? Where the hell have you been?"

It feels like forever since I've heard Dustin's voice, and as annoying as it is to hear—*still haven't forgiven you, mind you*—it's such a relief to know he's okay.

"Listen," I say, cutting to the point. "Are you guys looking for Eddie?"

"Yeah," he says. "And we found him—no thanks to you."

We who? I think, but there's no time. "You found him? Where?"

"A boathouse on Cole Mill Road—don't worry, he's safe. . . ."

"*Safe?* You guys know he killed Chrissy, right?" At least that's the current theory.

A pause, then: "That's bullshit. Eddie tried to *save* Chrissy."

"Then why do the cops all say he did it?"

There is a longer pause this time, then a voice comes on.

"Lucas, you're so behind, it's *ridiculous.*"

Max.

Just the sound of her voice, and the feeling that had been missing in my fingers returns, even jacks up to a tingling. *Max and Dustin, safe and together.* I couldn't have asked for more.

Max is still speaking. "Just meet us at school, and we'll explain everything."

I'm about to jump at the invitation before I remember where I am, what's waiting outside.

"I—I can't right now," I say. "I think some real bad shit's about to go down."

A loud rapping at the window jerks me back to the present, and I don't hear the rest of Max's question. I drop the receiver and turn.

Jason, Patrick, and Andy are standing at the window, staring hard at me.

I climb back out and join them, dread rising in my

chest. Their faces are set, angrier now that their journey's been made moot. Their eyes are laden with suspicion, watching me.

"The hell are you doing?" asks Jason.

Shit shit shit. I scramble through my brain for an answer, and the only thing I can come up with in the moment is: "Looking for . . . clues?"

They glance at one another, not amused. Jason's eyes narrow. The tension is thick enough to wring like a washcloth. Then Patrick chuckles and makes a joke about me being Sherlock Holmes, and the moment passes.

But then something strikes me. An *opportunity,* born of this very same lie. A way to both get back to my friends and prevent them from getting hurt.

"I found one."

They were already turning away, but they stop now, swivel back.

"A clue," I say. "I know where Eddie's hiding."

...

It's sundown by the time we arrive at the cabin in the woods. Jason pulls open his trunk, and I see even more items than the few I'd watched them gather back at Benny's Burgers: flashlights, hunting knives, a baseball bat, as if we're hunting monsters. If Jason's little dustup with Gareth is anything to go by, someone's about to get real hurt this time.

We grab our weapons of choice, Patrick and Andy choosing with wide-eyed delight, like kids at a candy store. I still have to prove myself to them, so I choose a weapon for myself as well—a tire iron.

Jason scratches out a plan on the ground in front of his headlights. He talks about *boxing the freak in* and gives directions on how we should advance, saying things like *flank his ass* and *the freak won't know what hit him*. I'm barely listening—I'm here for one thing and one thing alone.

We advance on the house, slowly. Patrick and Andy break off as planned, leaving Jason and me as the other team. Jason steps up to the front door, breathes, then kicks it in.

We rush in, just at the same time Andy and Patrick do, weapons out, ready to attack. But the place is empty. No Eddie, no Dustin, nobody.

"You sure this is the right place?" asks Jason.

"Positive," I say, trying to keep my eyes from betraying the familiarity of the place. The exact spot where the Spider Monster had attacked the cabin through the roof and left a hole in it. The exact place I'd climbed when I held that axe and chopped at its limb as it grabbed El's leg. The crumbled walls that were never fixed since Hopper died and El moved out of Hawkins with the Byerses.

I might be angry with my friends, and I might not care much for Eddie Munson, but there's no way on God's green earth that I'm going to allow Jason to hurt anyone again.

Too many people around me have been hurt already—Max, Jay, even Gareth. No more.

"Let's check around the back," Jason says to Andy and Patrick, infuriated. "Around the back!"

They head out, but I stand still, waiting for them to be caught up in that anger, to forget I'm here. Then I walk back out the way we came, slowly, then quickly.

I start to run.

. . .

Running won't take me very far, so my first stop is Hopper's outdoor shed. I shade the beam from the flashlight to prevent the boys from knowing that I'm here, while I search for what I hope is there. I find it easily.

Bingo. The small, shitty bike Hopper bought for El to learn how to ride, but which she never did. It's banged up and rusted now from lack of use, but the wheels still turn, and the chains still connect, and the brakes still work. That's all I need right now.

There's a mild squeaking when I push it out of the shed, but I'm sure the boys will have figured out the game by now. No use for stealth. I push the bike, hop on, and begin to pedal for my life.

Cycling with this flat-tire, rusted bike is harder than I thought—probably the hardest thing I've ever done. Much worse than running. But I keep on pedaling, keep on pushing. I think of it as penance for not paying enough attention all along, for allowing my anger to get the better of me. But I'm not angry anymore. I just want my friends to be safe.

I pedal faster, faster, my basketball cardio training finally coming through for me. Funny how things come around. Funny how basketball, Hellfire, Jay, Lee Garroway, Jason, and the team—all the things that happened this semester—have led up to this very moment: to help me see that staying true to those who have earned the title of *friend* is the most important thing after all. And now I have the tools—cardio and all—to prove it to them.

Cold wind blows into my face, wrenches tears from my eyes. Nothing else matters anymore. Not being popular, not basketball or the championship—not even high school. In this moment, getting back to Max and Dustin is all I want.

Max was right all along. The monsters in Hawkins don't always look like monsters. And the only thing that can save us from these monsters—be it Lee or Jason or the Mind Flayer—is sticking together. So I'm going to meet them at school, stick to them, and never let go.

I pedal faster, faster.

CHAPTER THIRTY-FIVE

SUNDAY, APRIL 6, 1986

It's pitch-dark night by the time I arrive at Hawkins High. The school is a silent, lifeless place at night, like a junkyard without cars. The parking lot, wide and empty, feels like it harbors ghosts. I dump my bike and head for the doors, scouting the area in hopes of finding Max or Dustin. No dice. Maybe they aren't here yet. Or they've already left?

I head for the main doors, hoping they'll easily find me there when they arrive. To my surprise, the doors are unlocked.

This is insane, I think, letting myself in.

The fluorescent lights above are out, and the hallway is even darker than outside. The pipes above crank noisily in the cold. It feels surreal, being back here like this. The last time I saw these hallways this empty—through the video-tape in my locker—a bomb had just been set off, and I was being interrogated. The last time I was here in person, it was the opposite—the halls were packed, and I was a hero being carried on shoulders. Who will I be tonight?

I bump into a vending machine. The sound echoes down the hallway. I curse under my breath and listen, wait-ing to hear if someone—maybe a janitor or something—is here. Nothing.

Vertigo hits me, and I shrug it off. Feels like I've been swinging between too many unreal things without pause for breath. Here I am, nerd turned cool kid, and the first time I walk the hallways is not to celebrate my newfound fame to high fives and cheers, but to break into school and help my friends avoid Satanist-hunting jocks. A lot of good being cool has done me so far, hasn't it?

I want to call out, hear if Max and Dustin are here, but I reconsider. Jason and the others could be lurking any-where.

But soon, I hear voices myself. Low, maybe conspirato-rial, but just sounding like someone trying not to be heard. I think I recognize Dustin's slight lisp, but there's another voice—*other voices?*—that I know isn't Max's.

Then a couple of flashlights come on, sweeping around me. Dustin's big hair comes into view.

I hurry forward, out of breath, dripping sweat and pray-ing I'm not wrong. Then—

Steve Harrington appears, swinging a weapon—*a lamp stand?*—and is about to bring it down on me.

"Whoa! Whoa! Whoa!" I put my hands over my head, skidding to a stop.

"Lucas?" a chorus of voices say, and it takes me a while to parse them out, for my eyes to adjust to the dim light, before I realize who else is here: *Robin. Nancy.*

"Jesus, dude!" says Steve. "What is wrong with you?"

"I've been biking for, like, *eight miles,*" I say, breathless. "We've got a *code red*!"

I push past Steve and grab Dustin by the shoulders and start telling him about Jason and Patrick and Andy and how he and Eddie are in danger, when he stops me.

It's then I notice the group's faces. Long, drawn, concerned. And they're not turned toward me. They're angled at the person standing away from us all, hovering around the front office.

Max.

Her eyes are wet with tears. And her face is ghost white. I've never seen her so scared.

• • •

On the ride to the Wheeler house in Steve's BMW, they fill me in.

The story, as Dustin tells it, is so bizarre that if anyone else heard us, they'd either call us bonkers or say we're living in some sort of fantasy world. I imagine if Jason and friends hear this, they'd feel immediately vindicated in their suspicions. And even though I completely disagree with their quest for retribution, I understand how they could be led astray.

Max saw something back in Forest Hills.

She doesn't speak the whole time, and I just watch her stare out the window in the back seat as Dustin describes it. Apparently, she showed up at Dustin's house this morning, breathless, panicked. First, she delivered a crucial bit of news: the police could be wrong, and she wasn't so sure Eddie Munson murdered Chrissy Cunningham. She'd seen them together the night of the game—Chrissy went into Eddie's trailer. *Odd,* Max had thought, and so do I, now, seeing as I remember Chrissy telling Jason she was going home to change for the party. Apparently, she was still wearing that outfit when she went into Eddie's trailer.

But then, the lights in Max's trailer flickered.

She looked out the window, wondering what was messing with the power, and saw Eddie drive off like a maniac. He looked mighty scared—also odd at the time, but not out of place for Eddie. But then the next day, the police came by. Max, loitering, managed a peek into the Munson trailer and saw Chrissy's body.

Dustin doesn't spare any details as he describes it secondhand. Limbs broken, facing opposite ways. Skin covered in dark, spiderweb-like veins. Ribs caved in, mouth wide open, frozen midscream. Eyes gouged, deep holes where they should be. Blood splattered on the ceiling of the trailer.

Max's conclusion was that either Eddie Munson was a really sick serial killer, or something else had killed Chrissy and scared Eddie off. Something *worse.*

After some sleuthing with phone calls and the lending register at Family Video—this is where Robin and Steve come in—they managed to trace Eddie to an out-of-town boathouse owned by some guy named Reefer Rick, who Eddie used to buy drugs from. They found him there, tucked away, hiding, scared.

He told them everything.

Eddie described Chrissy as being under a spell, and Dustin, the *one* person there who got to witness Will, Billy, and all the Flayed fall under the Mind Flayer's spell, put it together and knew immediately what had happened. Chrissy had been murdered by some sort of spellcasting dark wizard.

A wizard like Vecna.

Once Dustin says this name, memories of my first day at Hellfire come rushing back. *What are the odds!* Did some part of me *know,* back then, that something was brewing? In that brief moment wondering whether the Mind Flayer had a wizard of his own, did I sense him coming?

Vecna. I roll the name around my tongue. I knew this name was cursed from day one.

These guys, however, thought Eddie's description made no sense. Not at first. But then Fred Benson, Nancy's partner at the school paper, was found dead in the woods. Eyes gouged. Limbs snapped. Weblike veins all over his skin. Exactly like Chrissy.

It all clicked into place for them after that. They don't even need to tell me, at this point. As Dustin speaks, I already know it.

It's happening again. The gate is open. There's a killer on the loose in Hawkins, and it's not Eddie Munson.

But Dustin isn't done yet, because that's not the worst of it.

In trying to put the pieces together, Max figured out that both Chrissy and Fred had talked to the same counselor at school—Ms. Kelley. Which is how they'd ended up in school tonight, breaking into Ms. Kelley's office and searching her files. They confirmed it—both of them had files with the counselor, and both of them had described the same symptoms: terrible nightmares, cold sweats, insomnia, bad headaches, nosebleeds, visions, and trances.

Right now, there's one person having those *exact* symptoms who's still alive.

Max.

This is what they've been trying to gently ease me into all along: *Max is going to die.*

...

I don't speak for the rest of the ride to the Wheeler house. I spend it deep-diving into memories from that first day at Hellfire, unpacking each thought, each feeling upon seeing that painting of Vecna. Did I miss something I should have noticed—a sign of sorts? Was my constant worry for Max my sixth sense warning me that something was coming for her? Was this why I wanted to *be there* for her so much? Had I failed her by doing the opposite and giving her space?

Could I have stopped this?

It doesn't matter now, does it? It's here. Vecna is real, and he's in Hawkins, and we'll have to do something, or else. . . . Denial after denial flies through my brain. *No. Definitely not. Impossible.*

Max *cannot* die.

I watch her stare out the window. I want to reach out to her, comfort her. But she's even more withdrawn now. I remember the night we broke up, sitting in the cold at Elmore skatepark, and it suddenly feels like the best day of our lives. Bobbing our heads to Kate Bush, knowing that everything was ending. Even though there was pain, there was so much joy that night.

I'd give anything to have that back, over and over.

But by the time we get to the Wheelers' and all head down to the basement, I've decided: it's not over until it's over.

I told myself I needed to find my way back to Max, and I have. I've taken the roundabout route to it, paying attention to all the wrong things along the way—even trying to get her to come to a pointless game while her life was in danger! But there's no time to beat myself up about it. Every second counts now.

Max *cannot* die, and I will do everything in my power to keep her alive.

CHAPTER THIRTY-SIX

MONDAY, APRIL 7, 1986

Early next morning in the Wheeler basement, we get to work.

I make long-distance calls to Lenora Hills to fill El, Will, and Mike in on our situation. Part of me is hoping El can fly down to Hawkins as quickly as possible and deal with this Vecna dude with a snap of her fingers. But I call and call and no one picks up. I'm kinda upset because I think maybe they're out having fun—how can anyone have fun when Max is *dying*?

In the far corner of the basement, Max settles in at a workbench, scribbling a bunch of notes. Dustin asks me what she's writing, but I don't know, and I don't ask. She hasn't slept for the past twenty-four hours, and I don't blame her. If I was being hunted by a mind-attacking wizard from a parallel dimension, I wouldn't either. All I care about is keeping her alive.

I can't bear to consider the alternative. Look how the Party fell apart just by Will and El moving away. Losing Max would mean the end of everything. I can't even imagine what my own life would look like without her. Breaking up was different—I always knew she was out there somewhere, even if all wasn't always well with her. But *gone* gone? My chest hurts just trying to envision it. I turn my attention to the rest of the group.

Nancy, who'd been speaking to Wayne Munson, Eddie's uncle, before Fred's body was found, had found out that there was a serial murderer in Hawkins back in the fifties. After some digging in the Hawkins Public Library with Robin, they unearthed the guy's name: Victor Creel. Apparently, he was accused of murdering his own family, but he swore he'd been possessed by some demon and had no idea what he'd done.

A demon. Like Vecna.

Steve and Dustin are reading up on the Creel microfiche Nancy and Robin brought back from the library. We throw around theories about how Vecna's curse relates to Victor Creel. Apparently, the dude's still alive, holed up in some place called Pennhurst Asylum. Nancy and Robin head upstairs to try and figure out some way to reach him.

If they can talk to Victor, maybe he'll tell them how he escaped Vecna's curse, and then Max can too.

As much as I promised myself otherwise, I spend the rest of my time staring at Max. She hasn't had any further "episodes" yet—that's what Dustin's calling them. Apparently, she had one in the hallway back at school last night. She heard some sort of chime and saw a large grandfather clock. The group managed to snap her out of it. That's partly why they were all out in the hallway when I found them. But from what I've heard about what they saw in the files from Ms. Kelley's office, that episode is just the start. Chrissy's headaches lasted only a few weeks before she was killed. Fred's started just a week ago.

Max's headaches . . . *five days.*

She barely has twenty-four hours before the next episode. And if that episode comes, the chances that she'll survive it—slim to none.

■ ■ ■

Nancy and Robin have found a way to access Pennhurst Asylum and talk to Victor Creel.

After a few calls to her underlings at the school newspaper, Nancy has managed to snag fake résumés for her and Robin to pose as college students writing a thesis on paranoid schizophrenics. With these, they've managed to land a twelve o'clock with the director. They go upstairs and prepare to head out, Steve screaming after them, incensed that he's been left to "babysit" again.

In the small moment I have to breathe, I realize my parents haven't seen me since the night of the championship game. Whatever lie Erica's told has no doubt crumbled by now. Dad must be raging, and Mom's probably panicking, wondering if some Satanists have taken hold of me. I suspect they'll call the Wheeler house in no time, and for a moment, I wonder if I should preempt them to soften whatever punishment they have planned for me. I quickly decide against it, remembering Jason, Andy, and Patrick may still be out there looking for me and can show up at my house. If they do, I don't want my parents to unwittingly lead them here.

I return to worrying about Max. My parents' distress will just have to wait because I'm never letting Max out of my sight again. I did once before and look what happened. I know everyone here is looking out for each other, but no one's going to be as invested in Max's survival as I am. Just like Hopper with El, and Joyce with Will, I have to be the person she can depend on now.

Max finishes her last note, slips it into an envelope, and after catching me, Dustin, and Steve staring at her, packs them up and walks over to us. She hands Steve and Dustin an envelope each, and one for me. Then she passes me three more.

"Give these to Mike, El, and Will," she says. "If you ever get ahold of them again."

Dustin, trying to open his, asks her what's in them, but she stops him.

"It's just . . . a fail-safe," she says. "For after. If things . . . don't work out."

My heart skips a beat.

"Max," I say. "It's gonna wor—"

She shuts me down immediately. She doesn't *want* my reassurance.

"People have been telling me that my whole life," she says, "and it's almost never true."

She grabs the walkie and asks Dustin if it'll reach Pennhurst from East Hawkins, where the trailer park is. The answer is yes. So she starts up, heading out of the basement, Steve marching behind her.

I follow at a distance, holding the letters. My hands begin to shake.

Max and Steve argue as we head outside. Max is adamant that she'll not spend one more second of her possibly short life in the Wheeler basement, so we relent.

I keep my eyes on Max as we all climb into Steve's BMW. Right before she enters, Max pauses, turns, and stares off into the distance. It's a small action, but from the fear that crosses her face, I know, immediately, that she's heard those chimes again.

Vecna is *coming*.

■ ■

On the ride to Max's trailer, I continue watching her look out the window. I hold back on making the joke that comes to mind, pointing out the irony of the situation: of course the first time she invites me over to her new place, it's because she's dying. The joke's humor catches in my throat as I realize I may not be wrong.

This might be the last time I see Max.

The good times we've had together come flashing through to me. The first time we met alone in that back room at the arcade, when she didn't believe me. Our first kiss, at the Snow Ball. The early parts of the summer of Starcourt, before it all went to shit. We wore matching shirts and made inside jokes and bought a ton of Scoops Ahoy and set off fireworks and saw a bunch of horror movies. She tried to teach me how to skate, and I sucked at it, but that was okay. We argued and broke up and got back together and ribbed each other. We cried when El and the Byerses left. She tried to run away to California last Halloween, and I sat with her in silence. We broke up, and I sat with her in silence.

I clutch the letter. I will sit with her in silence. Right until the very end.

CHAPTER THIRTY-SEVEN

MONDAY, APRIL 7, 1986

Steve's BMW pulls up at the Forest Hills trailer park. Max gets out and hurries toward a trailer I'm guessing is hers. She's going to hand out one of those letters to her mom. I told her it'll only complicate matters, but Max was adamant.

Steve tells her to hustle up, but she ignores him. As we wait in the silence, I take a moment to look around. For some reason, it doesn't look as shitty as everyone describes. It's just a bunch of trailers, and while I'd probably not live in one if I had a choice, I can't say it's the worst thing in the world.

Max dying—*that's* the worst thing in the world.

A few moments later, the car door jerks open, and Max is back. Except—she's breathless again, and there are tears in her eyes.

"Did something happen?" I ask.

"Just drive," she says, and I know what that means.

We're running out of time.

• • •

It's nearing sundown by the time Max directs us to our final destination: the Hawkins Cemetery.

Just like earlier, she jumps out of the car and begins to head up the hill. But it's too much for me. First all these opaque letters, and now she's heading into a . . . *cemetery*? I can't bear this anymore.

I jump out and follow her. After a while, she clocks that I'm following her and turns around.

"Lucas, please just stay in the car," she says.

"I know something happened back there," I say. "With your mom."

Guilt flashes across her face. I was right.

"Was it . . . Vecna?" I press.

"I told you, I'm fine," she insists. "I mean, as fine as someone who's hurtling toward a horrific death can be. . . ." She lets out a small, unconvincing chuckle.

"Max," I say, "you know you can talk to me, right?"

I'm hoping it works this time. The last time I tried this

300

approach, she wasn't dying. Right now, anything will do, if it'll just get her to look me in the eye and *let me help her.*

She pauses. Looks like it's working.

"Yeah," she says. "I know that."

"Then why are you pushing me away?" I hold up the letter marked with my name. "I don't need a letter. Or *want* a letter. Just—talk to me. To your friends. We're right here." I poke a hand to my chest. *"I'm right here."*

She watches me carefully. A breakthrough. For the first time in a long time, I feel like I'm finally crossing the mountain. I'm finally getting through to Max. It would be exhilarating if it wasn't under such dire circumstances. I can see her lips part, ready to open herself up, to find her way back to me just like I've found mine to her.

Then, at the last second, she says:

"This won't be long. Just—wait in the car."

Then she trudges up the hill and leaves me standing there, letter in hand.

■ ■ ■

Steve Harrington gets impatient real quick, and there's no stopping him when he's there.

I'm barely back in the car for twenty minutes before he decides Max has spent enough time in a graveyard filled with dead bodies. He gets out and hustles up the hill to her.

I watch as he tries to get her to get up from where she's

kneeling. At first, he just looks impatient. Then his body language changes, and he kneels before her.

I call Dustin. Steve starts to shake Max, but her body remains limp. My heart pounds faster as it dawns on me what's happening.

The final episode. She's under Vecna's curse.

Dustin and I leap out of the car and race up the hill. We arrive at the grave—which turns out to be Billy Hargrove's—next to her envelope marked: *To Billy.* Max is now lying on the ground, her eyes fluttering quickly—a trance.

Dustin, Steve, and I shake her as much as we can.

"Max!" we scream. "Max! Wake up!"

"Robin—Nancy!" says Steve. "Call them!"

Dustin sprints back down the hill, cursing the whole way. Steve and I try as much as we can to wake her up. No dice. She remains limp, noncompliant, like a battleship commandeered.

I look down the hill and see Dustin screaming into the walkie. *Please have a solution,* I pray. *Please have a solution.* Turning back to Max, I try to think about what I might say that'll bring her back.

"Max," I say, panic choking my words. "Please, wake up. I promise to be better—I'll do whatever you want; I'll quit the team if I have to. I'll be a better boyfriend. I'll see the movies you want, play the games you want. I'll follow you to California if you want me to. I'll learn how to skate and wear board shorts and wear Jeff Spicoli sneakers, I promise. But please just wake up!"

Her eyes keep fluttering, succumbing to Vecna's curse.

Dustin hustles back up the hill, cradling a bunch of items. I want to scream at him—*What are you doing with a Walkman—she's dying!* But then he dumps them before me.

"Her song," he says, out of breath. "Do you know her favorite song?"

"What?!" I say, almost incensed. "Why?"

"Robin said that—" He decides against explaining. "It's too hard to explain, just—what's her favorite song?!"

Without needing another invite, I dig into the mass of cassette tapes before me. There's a bunch of other new music I haven't seen before, but my mind barely registers the names. All I'm looking for is the one cassette that matters.

Please be here, please be here.

I spot the purple album art—Kate Bush holding two dogs, hair splayed wildly across the floor. I grab the cassette, plunk it into the Walkman without checking if it's rewound. Dustin places the earphones over her ears.

Please work, please work.

I push play.

The drums to "Running Up That Hill" begin to sound, a tinniness far away. We continue tugging at her, trying to get the music to do whatever magic it's supposed to do faster. In my mind, I pray my own prayer.

Come back to me, Max, I think. *Come back to me.*

Then something happens. Max's eyes stop fluttering.

She starts to lift off the ground, up in the air. Levitating.

In Eddie Munson's description of what happened to Chrissy, levitation was the beginning of the end. Before her limbs snapped and her eyes were sucked inside their sockets, she levitated.

Steve, Dustin, and I back away in horror. I feel like a part of me is tearing away, slipping out of reach. *Max is going to die* is the only thought on my mind. *Max is going to die.*

It feels like forever that she's suspended in the air, Kate Bush playing as if from far, far away. She rises, rises, and all I can think about is what my life will be like without her, what I could've done to protect her. It took being away from her to finally find a way to myself, to discover all the parts I'd overlooked. I've become better for it. Now that change has to find its way to Max, so she can be better too. But she must stay alive for that to happen.

Don't die, I whisper to myself. Max has always been my guiding light, my North Star. Finding my way back to her was really finding my way back to me.

Don't die, I whisper, *because I don't want to be alone again.*

Max drops to the ground with a thump.

We rush over. My eyes are already filling with tears as I kneel next to her, Steve checking her pulse. Everything is so blurred, all I can do is listen. For the sound of breath, of her voice saying she's okay. *Just wake up, please.* I wipe my eyes and listen harder than I've ever done. Is this what Robin meant all this time about paying attention? Is this what I get for not doing that enough?

Please wake up, I think. *I will listen better. I promise.*

Then, as if she's heard me, Max opens her eyes and gasps for air.

Her face is so white—scared down to her bones. She chokes back tears, trying to speak, to make words out of feelings she has no words for. I have no words either, only overwhelming joy. I nearly can't believe it. *Kate Bush worked!*

I scoop her into my arms, tears running down my cheeks. In this moment, everything feels complete, like we have come full circle. Kate Bush was there when we fell apart, and now Kate Bush has brought her back to me.

"I thought we lost you," I say.

"I'm still here," Max replies, wrapping her arms tight around me, her voice weighty with tears and joy and relief. "I'm still here."

Lucas's guide to surviving freshman year:

- ☑ Make new friends
- ☑ Get out of comfort zone and try new things
- ☑ ~~Be yourself~~ It's okay to be different
- ☑ Avoid relationship and friendship drama
- ☑ Remember to live in the moment
- ☑ Help my friends

SAVE HAWKINS, SAVE MAX.

ACKNOWLEDGMENTS

My sincere thanks go to . . .

My editorial team at Penguin Random House: Thanks for always providing a cushion throughout the topsy-turvy period from this book's inception to its completion. Sara Sargent: for standing as a seamless bridge between the book and TV teams. Lois Evans: for all those long afternoons brainstorming over Zoom and for providing the structure that eventually powered this novel through. This book is as much yours as mine.

Eddie Schneider, my agent: for your innate ability to fashion calm from chaos.

The *Stranger Things* team at Netflix: for offering me the opportunity to give our beloved tough, thoughtful, and sincere Black nerd from Hawkins the story he deserves.

The Duffer Brothers: for creating this world and these characters, without whom Lucas and our merry band of rule breakers would not exist.

Caleb McLaughlin: for bringing the character of Lucas

to life with such verve; for giving us a seat at the table; for containing multitudes.

My partner, Dami: for holding space for Dot and me during the crazed period in which I wrote this book. Your support, as always, is invaluable.

All *Stranger Things* nerds and readers out there: this is for you.

© 2020 Manuel Ruiz

SUYI DAVIES is a Nigerian author of fantasy and science fiction. He has written a number of works for younger readers, including *Minecraft: The Haven Trials*. He was a contributor to the instant #1 *New York Times* bestselling middle-grade anthology *Black Boy Joy*. He lives in Ontario, Canada, where he is a professor of English at the University of Ottawa.

suyidavies.com